Larkspur

Happily Ever After

Melody
JEN MELLAND

Larkspur
KELSEY KILGORE

Evie
HILARY HAMBLIN

KELSEY KILGORE

HAPPILY EVER AFTER

Larkspur

Broadstreet Publishing
2745 Chicory Road, Racine, WI 53403
Broadstreetpublishing.com

Published in partnership with **OakTara Publishers, www.oaktara.com**

Cover design by Yvonne Parks at www.pearcreative.ca
Cover and interior design © 2014 by OakTara Publishers
Cover images © shutterstock.com: beautiful woman smiling cheerfully/auleena, 112062878; © thinkstockphotos.ca: green grass over sunlight/oksix, 466347305
Author photo © Kelsey Kilgore

Larkspur, © 2014, Kelsey Kilgore; © 2014, 2008 as *A Love for Larkspur*, by Kelsey Kilgore. Scripture taken from the HOLY BIBLE, NEW INTERNATIONAL VERSION®. NIV®. Copyright © 1973, 1978, 1984 by International Bible Society. Used by permission of Zondervan. All rights reserved.

All rights reserved. No part of this publication may be reproduced, stored in a retrieval system, or transmitted in any form or by any means without the prior written permission of the publisher. The only exception is brief quotations in professional reviews.

ISBN-13: 978-1-4245-9906-6 • ISBN-10: 1-4245-9906-7
eISBN-13: 978-1-4245-9907-3• eISBN-10: 1-4245-9907-5

Larkspur is a work of fiction. References to real people, events, establishments, organizations, or locales are intended only to provide a sense of authenticity and are used fictitiously. All other characters, incidents, and dialogue are drawn from the author's imagination. The perspective, opinions, and worldview represented by this book are those of the author and are not intended to be a reflection or endorsement of the publishers' views.

Printed in the U.S.A.

For my family

With affection and gratitude
for all your love and support

"Why don't you meet guys at school or at your jobs, again?"

This is only the hundredth time Mama's asked me this. She doesn't know that I *am* highly motivated to meet someone. *The* Someone, if you will. So motivated that I secretly scan the personals from time to time, but there's no need to confess that to her, or to anyone else.

"You need help meeting quality men. *Prescreened* men. So I'm going to screen men for you, and that way you'll only have to go out with the ones that I approve first. I'll weed out the creeps."

"How nice." And, in theory, it does sound nice. But in the reality playing out in my head, *Oh, God help me....*

1

"You want me to cut your hair?" Mama checks her reflection in the mirror, sucking in her cheeks to create the illusion of cheekbones.

"Why would I want you to do that? You don't even know how!" I remind her. She has apparently tired of watching me repeatedly blow a too-long strand off my forehead.

"Could if I tried," she says.

I doubt it, but it's just hair. "Sure."

Mama goes to the kitchen drawer and gets a pair of scissors I saw her cut raw chicken with last week. I don't say anything, though, because chicken germs probably don't hang around for a week anyway. And it's just hair.

I sit on the toilet and watch pieces of strawberry blond fall to the beige linoleum.

"I have a plan I need to tell you about."

I wish she didn't have scissors in her hands. Mama gets wild plans. That she's telling me about one while cutting, and that she needs to tell me about this one—well, neither one of those is good.

"Sure."

"I read in the newspaper that Plains Point has twice the available men your age as they do young women. I can't remember why that is, but that's what it said."

"Uh-huh." I doubt her statistic is correct but don't bother to say so.

"Men should be scrambling to get dates then."

"Haven't seen any scramble my way in a long time, Mama."

"I know! That's my point, baby."

Yeah, I'm 26, but Mama still calls me that. I think it's cute, really. Better than my real name.

1

LARKSPUR

"So...your plan?" I'm cringing, partly because the scissors are dull, and she's having to saw a little with them.

"Why don't you meet guys at school or at your jobs, again?"

This is only the hundredth time Mama's asked me this. She doesn't know that I *am* highly motivated to meet someone. *The* Someone, if you will. So motivated that I secretly scan the personals from time to time, but there's no need to confess that to her, or to anyone else.

"Mama, I do meet guys. But the ones who ask me out aren't believers, or if they are, they're creepy, and I always say no."

"How can a nice brother in the Lord be creepy?"

I can't help but smile at the "brother in the Lord" phrase. I think she even said it with a straight face. "Last week a guy came into Java, The Hut in a three-piece suit and a tie with a big cross on it. He said he had been awakened in the night with a vision of asking out the first girl he spoke with that day."

"Well, that's not...*so* bad." Her scissors stop, blades wide apart while she thinks. "He could have had that vision."

"No, he did not! He went on to whip out a bottle of oil and ask if he could first anoint my head before asking me to dinner."

I have my head down, but I can see the front of Mama's black dress shake like she's holding in a laugh.

"Can I ask what you were wearing?"

"The black T-shirt with the words, *Jesus will save your sorry butt.*"

"I think that's what did it."

"Yeah, me too. But 'brothers in the Lord' can be creepier than you think. I'd like to find a nice one, though."

"Okay, so you need help meeting quality men. *Prescreened* men."

"Uh-huh." I shift on the blue fuzzy toilet seat cover. "Would have been good to have a personal Man Screener that day."

"Exactly! I have more free time than you do, and I know how to meet men."

"You what?"

"How do you think I met Stanley?"

"Oh, right." Stanley is Mama's second husband—a real sweetheart who is so quiet I tend to forget him. But he's a good guy, I'll give her that.

"Sit still, and lean your head this way a little. So I'm going to screen men for you, and that way you'll only have to go out with the ones that I approve first. I'll weed out the creeps."

"How nice." And, in theory, it does sound nice. But in the reality playing out in my head, *Oh, God help me.* Mama sending me the door-to-door vacuum salesman, or the guy at the bank who insists on sending me lollipops through the cash carrier. Or every single guy she talks to in the course of her day—and Mama talks to everybody. I can just hear it now: "Lark, I set up a date for you with the guy who held open the door for me at the post office." Oh, it could happen like that. Easily, knowing Mama.

Mama smiles at me. "I hoped you'd go for it."

"Um, do you think many will pass your screening? I mean, you can be pretty particular." Really, I'm afraid she'll overlook every single guy I'd actually like and send me on dates with all the ones I'd never consider. I can totally see her setting me up with losers by the herd, but rejecting all the hundreds of attractive, available men mentioned in the newspaper article.

"Well, that makes it that much better for you." Mama stops and checks her reflection again in the mirror. She turns her head slightly to each side, then returns to me with the scissors. "I won't pass anyone on to you that I wouldn't want for a son-in-law. What other qualities are you looking for?"

"Believer, denomination unimportant, but must have a very low creep factor, regardless of spiritual belief."

"Good one. Okay, how cute does he have to be?"

"I don't think that matters much. I don't think I'm too cute myself, right now, Mama." But I've always been such a dork over the really cute ones. Then I find out that they're flamingly gay or greatly conceited—with good reason, of course. Given the correct circumstances, I could totally be a fool for Tom Cruise, Scientology, and all. Poor Katie, she really needed Mama. Blinded by cuteness, we can all go *so* wrong.

Which reminds me to ask how wrong my hair has gone. "You about ready to stop cutting?"

Mama steps back and looks at me, and I can tell it hasn't gone how she envisioned. "Well, maybe I should. I'd pictured a haircut that Ashley Judd had in the movie I watched last night, but this isn't it."

Oh my gosh. If I'd known that, I would have stopped her. I look like a bad Peter Pan. Hair is hacked and sticking up in various lengths all over my head. If I were Ashley Judd, or any other Hollywood actress, maybe I could pull it off. Well, no, not even then. But I'm a freckle-faced Texas girl with too many jobs, and this haircut has the words *white trash* written all over it.

I sigh. "Thanks, Mama."

"It's just hair, baby."

Sure. Just hair. Like there weren't a half-dozen magazine articles on how to have hair like Katie Holmes in the weeks leading up to Tom's Eiffel tower proposal. Just hair.

"Yeah, find me a man who doesn't care about pretty hair. Maybe one of those guys who really thinks Sinead O'Connor is hot. Are there any of those guys?"

"Maybe in the nineties, there were. But I'll be sure to ask all the men I meet." She's kidding, so I try to ignore it. That would be easy, except that I can actually see her asking random men if they're more attracted to Julia Roberts or to Sinead O'Connor. I plant a kiss on her plump cheek and rush out the door for a shift at the Laun-dro-matio. It's completely lame, but I get to study a lot while I'm there, and I'm never behind on my laundry.

I can't help but note that my mother managed to diminish my physical appearance, while at the same time plan how to get me a man. Interesting approach, I'll give her that. My cell phone rings, and it's her, even though I'm barely out of the driveway.

No hello. "I need to know what nights each week you can keep free for this project."

The Man Getting Project, I assume. "Wednesday and Friday."

"Don't you have singles class at church on Wednesdays?"

"No, they were a bad influence on me." I never bothered to explain that the singles class was far more interested in dating one another than in anything having to do with God. And, really, that could be a good thing considering I need someone to date…except it wasn't. Nothing like going to church and feeling like you've done something worse for your spiritual self than if you'd stayed home and played Cake Mania for hours on your laptop. I just don't need that kind of guilt.

"Okay, Lark, I love you and don't you worry about what you look like."

"Thanks, Mama. I…wasn't." But now I am. I hang up, reaching for my slightly wavy spikes. Even Meg Ryan couldn't pull this look off.

Ross nods in acknowledgment, glad to see me so that he can leave the Laun-dro-matio. He is wearing all black, as usual, and his nose piercing looks different today, but I can't tell why.

"I like the hair. It's punker than I thought you were."

"Yeah, but not punker than Mama."

He just looks at me like he doesn't understand what I said and waves with two fingers as he leaves. The place is empty, so I spread out my books and sit on one of the big folding tables.

I've been there for long enough to have a cramp in my neck when Brant Stephens walks by. I roll my eyes at the khakis and denim shirt he wears, extra starch.

We went to school together—elementary, not college. Brant has more degrees than I can remember and more annoying personality flaws than I can count. He lives down the street, on the other side, and he sometimes runs in the mornings when I do. It's an unfortunate occurrence, and on those mornings we exchange a few insults when we pass—a game that used to be more fun.

He thinks I'm nobody, and I think he's an overrated somebody. He had scholarships and tuition handed to him, and I can't blame him for not being able to relate to me. I work two low-paying jobs—three if you count my living arrangements. I do yardwork and errands for my landlady, and in return I pay a very low rent for the one-bedroom apartment in her backyard.

Besides working at the Laun-dro-matio, I work at the campus bookstore. I am the Minimum Wage Queen, and no job is beneath me. I kind of like that about me, actually.

I've taken classes for too many years at the local community college and have no intention of earning a degree. I simply take the courses I think I might need one day, regardless of how they fit into a degree plan.

LARKSPUR

Which isn't smart, especially since I've been harboring a secret desire to become an accountant. But it sounds so dull, and so not me that I'm in denial of it. I think of myself as more lively than any accountant could ever be, so I hesitate in rushing in that direction. I consider myself more of a firefighter, or private detective sort. Not that those jobs appeal to me, but they possess the "glam quality" that accounting doesn't have.

I've finished kneading the knots out of my neck when Brant sticks his head in the door. I was hoping he wouldn't. He's been at the dry cleaners next door and has an armful of clear-bagged preppie clothes.

"Hey, Lark, you looked like you were dragging a little this morning. Feeling out of shape?"

"Nah, only short on sleep." I don't attempt to return the slam, since I know he's going to notice my hair any minute. This is not an insult-fest I can win, so I play sweet.

He steps inside and lets the door shut behind him with a bang. "Hey, do you remember that cat I had when we were younger? The one with the skin disease that made her scratch all the time?"

I remember. "Yeah."

"That's what you remind me of today, Lark. Her fur stood up just like that."

I have no comeback. I can't even play sweet anymore. I smile, sort of, and look at the door. My neck tenses up again.

Something flashes across his face, and I think he's about to apologize. Even that was meaner than our usual exchanges. He smiles back, showing his perfect teeth, and walks out. No apology. The door bangs closed, and I watch him carefully hang his preppie clothes on the hook in the back of his silver Mercedes. That has to be the most boring, predictable man on earth. Then again, they said that about BTK, and he turned out to be a serial killer. Brant couldn't even have a surprising side to his personality, much less a dangerous one. And this is why for at least the last five years I've thought of him as Boring Brant.

I stare blankly at my books, depressed at the thought of resembling anybody's out of shape, sick cat, now long dead. Any flicker of hope that I might, with Mama's help, be on the verge of meeting *The* Someone, totally vanishes. I am ill-suited to attract anyone at all if I remind Brant of that particular cat. His cat easily made the one in *Sweet Home Alabama* look healthy. You know, the one that had been set on fire and survived a few explosions? The worst part is that he wasn't just being mean. I remember that cat, and there is a frightening similarity.

Hours pass with that thought in the back of my mind, as I sit alone in the Laun-dro-matio. I'm studying a chapter on tax laws for my current accounting course, which I've found doesn't require all of my brain to be present anyway. Maybe I'll become a brilliant accountant in a country in which a woman's hair is unimportant, and the locals find it a highly exciting, glamorous career.

It's nice to see Gloria, who has the next shift, since her arrival means I can walk out into the bright evening, instead of sitting behind glass. There's something about this part of West Texas, even in March, that makes the evening sun turn everything golden and pretty, so it's good to be out here. This square of businesses is my very small world. The Laun-dro-matio sits on one side, with the dry cleaners next door, and that side faces the florist shop, Rosie's Posies, and the Save-Some grocery store. On another side of the square are the Coffee Café—café mochas that rival Starbucks and are way cheaper—and Hazel's Hair Haven. I've never been to Hazel's, but she's probably better than Mama.

There are other businesses that open and close after a few months, and I don't keep tabs on those. Two blocks behind the Coffee Café is where I live, in Mrs. Huttle's backyard apartment. She's a grouch of an old woman, and she likes me to do what she wants without having to speak to me. Mind-reading required for that role.

I head to Coffee Café for a café mocha but never get there. A woman standing outside Hazel's Hair Haven stamps out a cigarette, and when I pass her, she reaches out to touch my elbow. I jump. I didn't expect that.

"Hi there." She's holding my arm and looking at my hair, and I am suddenly back in the hallway of elementary school and a teacher is trying to determine if I have a hall pass. I decide these dynamics are unacceptable and reach out and hold her by the elbow, too. It would have been better to pull away, but this lady is almost as big as Mama, and I don't think I'd get away if she didn't want me to. So now we're just strangers, standing there in a weird half embrace, and that's not what I was going for either.

LARKSPUR

Still holding her arm, I say, "Hi."

She shrugs me off with ease, opens the door to Hazel's, pulling me in, while never taking her eyes off my hair. "Honey, it looks like you got attacked by some really dull-bladed pruning shears. I'm Hazel, and I will help you." She's talking slowly, as if to an accident victim about to go into shock. And she thinks that is clearly the appropriate state of mind for someone with hair like mine.

"Okay, Hazel. They were my mama's kitchen shears, and you can help me, but I don't have any money on me today."

"You don't have to pay me—this is my good deed for society, honey." I'm in her blue vinyl chair, and I start to ask if she wants to know what I'd like it to look like when she's done, but I don't. There are probably not a lot of options left anyway.

Hazel snips away, muttering about kitchen shears, too involved in her mission for small talk. Which is fine with me. Despite my being grabbed on the sidewalk, Hazel is kind of nice, and I decide that her heart must be very giving, to go to so much trouble for a stranger. Then she starts cursing, having found a particularly short patch. Well, you can have a mouth like a sailor and still have a giving heart, I suppose.

"This here?" She points to the patchy part behind my left ear, and I nod in acknowledgment. "Only time can heal this, honey."

Isn't that a lyric from a Cher song?

"You come back when it grows out, and I'll even it out for you." She shakes her head from side to side, continuing her work. I wonder if small talk is only for paying customers, or if Hazel even does small talk. This is such a far cry from the beauty parlor scenes in *Steel Magnolias*, but it doesn't matter. I look so much more fabulous than I thought I could with short hair and a patchy spot. Short wisps of strawberry blond decorate my head, and I am so glad Hazel grabbed me. I am chic and sophisticated and modern, except that it's still just me. However, it's pretty hot, considering what it looked like an hour ago.

"You work around here, don't you?" Hazel asks.

I fill her in on my jobs and she gives me a pat. "Good for you. A hard worker. I like that. You come see me when you need a trim, and if you ever need another job."

I look around the deserted place, wondering if Hazel needs any help. But I thank her anyway and even give her a hug. She laughs and follows me out to light another cigarette and maybe accost another worthy pedestrian.

I grab the phone on the second ring as I carefully tiptoe across the carpet to avoid getting carpet fuzz on my pedicure. I've just arrived home, checked Hazel's amazing repair work for the third time in the mirror, and painted my toenails Pink Kiss.

"Hey, Lark, can I come over?"

It's Christine, long-time friend and fellow nail-polish enthusiast—which we regularly trade. "Sure."

"Great, I need help putting together a jogging stroller."

Christine is my age and single, and this makes no sense. "Is there something you want to tell me?"

"Yeah, I got a job! See ya in a minute!"

And she hangs up without explaining why she's putting together a jogging stroller, or even what that might be.

I meet her out in front of Mrs. Huttle's, and we haul in parts and tools together, making it in one trip.

"So this is for what?"

"You know Marilyn, the lady I babysit for sometimes? She's pregnant with her second kid, and her doctor put her on bedrest."

"Uh huh. And this is hers?" I put the stroller pieces on the step in front of my door, noting that it isn't completely unassembled. This is a good thing, or we'd be at it for hours.

"Yeah, her 'extra.' Marilyn was the StrollerMama instructor, but she can't be now, of course."

"What's a StrollerMama instructor?"

"You know, those moms who meet at parks and at the mall and they do workouts as a group, and they all have their kids in strollers."

"So you're the new StrollerMama?" I laugh at her. Hard.

"Yes! What's so funny?"

"You're not a mom, and I bet this is the closest you ever came to a stroller."

"So? I did aerobics at the Y one summer! I can instruct a bunch of moms to walk, while doing knee lifts, and encourage proper breathing."

"Sure. You're right, you can."

Christine flips her long, straight brown ponytail behind her shoulder. "And I'll be really positive. I plan on quoting Scriptures to them pertaining to motherhood. Like, 'Your children shall rise up and call you blessed.'"

"Good luck with that."

Christine is making great headway on stroller assembly, and I wonder why she thought she needed my help in the first place.

"Next week you can decide to be a midwife if this doesn't work out."

I hand her a tube-shaped part and she asks, "What's Mama up to?"

"Finding me a man."

"Goooood! If anyone can, it's her. Sorry, didn't mean it like that."

"It's fine. I've been thinking the same thing. Don't you think, though, that it'll be tough?"

"No, why?"

"Maybe I've been watching too much TV or flipping through too many *People* mags, but I'm pretty sure great hair and boobs are still 'in.'"

"Uh huh." Christine reaches for a part, and I scoot it closer with my foot.

"So, in today's society, these are the appropriate man-getting tools. In case you haven't noticed, I don't have them. How in the world are you supposed to get a guy without hair and boobs, when every other woman out there has them and flaunts them?"

"What about Kate Hudson?"

"Gorgeous, and gorgeous hair, if not the rest."

"What about attracting just one man? *The* man? I mean, why do you need to attract all kinds of guys, when you're only looking for one?"

I hesitate before asking, "How can you attract even one, if his tongue is falling out of his mouth and his eyes are glazed over by all the cleavage on everyone else? Every single commercial, TV show, and magazine can't be wrong when they indicate that breasts are still all the rage, and of great importance to your average joe." I look down at my chest and back at Christine. "Did you ever watch that show?"

"What show?" Christine isn't known for her attention span.

"*Average Joe.*"

"No."

"Oh. It was okay. Not as trashy as a lot of reality TV."

I raise my eyebrows, waiting to see if she'll remember what we're talking about. She spins a wheel with her foot. "But you don't want your 'average joe.' God will make you absolutely irresistible to The One. You know, set you apart in a way that can't be missed. And it won't be hard. You're too pretty to be talking like this."

"Yeah. I'll look like those early religious paintings. When the artists wanted to show that their representation of Jesus was the true Christ, they'd paint a yellow half circle behind his head, like a bright firefly was always buzzing behind him. You know the paintings I mean?"

"Right. You think God will give you a firefly glow?"

"No, I'd rather He give me breasts, but I don't think that's happening, suddenly, at age 26, either."

"Sarah thought she was too old and look what happened to her." Christine gives me a knowing look.

I can't think of any Sarah that we know, but Christine won't stop with the knowing, nodding look. And then, because it's Christine and I understand her weird mind, I get it. And that's the only reason. "*Sarah?* As in the woman who had Isaac at, like, age 100? *That's* who you're comparing me to?"

"No! Not at all. Well, yeah, but I didn't think it through first." Christine giggles as only she can. It makes her sound like she's five, with a secret. "I know!" Christine stares at me. Clearly she has a great idea. "What about a Miracle Bra?"

Ah, and this just shows how much she doesn't get my predicament. "Christine, I'm *wearing* a Miracle Bra!"

"*Really?* Huh." And she can't help but laugh, and I don't blame her.

"You about done with that?"

"Yeah, you've been an amazing help," she says sarcastically. "What happened to your hair anyway? It's cute."

LARKSPUR

"Mama cut it. Then a lady grabbed me on the street and fixed it so it didn't look so bad."

"Yeah, sure, Lark." She doesn't believe me, but I let it go.

"Pray for me tomorrow, and I'll call and tell you how it goes." She walks off with her newly assembled jogging stroller, doing high knee lifts.

"You go, Mom!"

I was going to give her Pink Kiss to take home, but my phone rings and Mama sounds out of breath on the other end. "Larkspur!"

I hate it when she calls me that.

"I have two fantastic men who are meeting you for coffee tonight. Meet Jason at 7 o'clock at Coffee Café, and meet Jim right after that at 7:30."

"Tonight?" How in the world did she meet two fantastic men since lunchtime? I've never met two fantastic men, well, ever. I wonder what Mama's version of fantastic men is. An image of Stanley, my stepfather, in his one-piece, belted work suit comes to mind. Hmm. And she met *two* this quickly?

"Yes, tonight. You said you were free on Wednesdays and Fridays, and today is Wednesday."

"I know, but I didn't think you meant *now*!"

"Well, it worked out that way, baby. And wear a skirt. You have my legs, you know." *Click.*

I wonder at that combination of advice. Mama has legs like tree trunks. Like hundred-year-old redwoods that cars could drive through because they're so wide. And then the conflicting "so wear a skirt." Conflicting in the same way as giving me the sick-cat haircut and then announcing it's time to attract men. But that's Mama.

I run to the bathroom, because if I don't shave I'm going to have legs so furry they'll remind another man of his cat.

2

So I'm sitting in Coffee Café with incredible hair, hairless legs, and a skirt, fervently praying that the guy who walked in is my date. This is not your typical Plains Point guy. I've never seen guys who looked like this one except maybe in magazines or on TV. *Wow.* I know what it is: it's like the hottest guy ever, straight from the pages of the latest J.Crew catalog. No kidding. (And no, I don't shop J.Crew on my income, but I do like the catalogs.) Somehow, prayers are answered. J.Crew comes over and offers the most amazing lopsided smile and asks if I'm Lark.

"I am." It comes out all breathy. I'm so thankful Mama didn't tell him my name is Larkspur. I notice the five-ish shadow on his jawline is a few shades lighter than the dark, dark hair on his head.

Surprisingly, the chemistry is two-way. *Thank You, God, and thank you, Mama!*

J.Crew sits across from me, and we talk and laugh and stare. I hate it that he's the first of my two dates and that he's already said that he knows he only has 30 minutes with me. If he were the next guy, we'd be closing down Coffee Café.

Somewhere about halfway through our half hour he nervously reaches across the table and places his hand next to mine, so some of our fingers are touching. He isn't holding my hand, but it's almost. It's pretty good, and I realize it's been such a long time since I've had a date that even a little finger brushing is nice.

J.Crew talks a lot about freedom and independence and looks so sincere and gorgeous that I merely nod and agree and lean closer across the table. I think he's talking about freedom in Christ, but I'm really not listening. I'm issuing silent praises to my benevolent Father in heaven, who has clearly worked all things together for my good. Oh, I love it when Scripture makes sense!

LARKSPUR

He has to leave way too soon, but he asks me to go to a rally with him on Saturday and I almost yelp "yes!" He gives me his card, and I stand, hoping irrationally for a kiss from this beautiful man whom I will surely marry and whose name I cannot remember.

He doesn't kiss me, but he does give me one of those memorable, lopsided smiles and asks if I will call him tomorrow.

Oh yes, I will call him. And in the meantime, I must not fantasize over a man I have just met. Oh, call it what it is, Lark. I must not *lust* over a man I have just met. Even if he is my future husband. I must not lust, I must not lust.

I sit down, fingers tingling, and don't notice anyone enter until a long-haired blond guy sits down across from me and offers his hand to shake. "I'm Jim." He gives a nod and a wink at the same time, and before I can introduce myself, he gets up and walks to the counter. He didn't ask if I wanted anything, but he returns with two plastic stir sticks, not drinks.

He beats out a rhythm on the edge of our table. His eyes are closed and he's really into it, so I wait for a while, then go order a café mocha, and return to my seat in time for him to finish. He clearly is the drummer for some high-energy rock band, and he looks spent, as if he's finished a really long concert. I decide not to dwell on the fact that this was a stir-stick performance on the edge of a table, and the heaving, out-of-breath routine he's doing is garnering attention I wish it weren't. I'm a little judgmental, probably, since no one could measure up to J.Crew.

"I'm Lark."

"I'm a drummer. I thought you would want to immediately become enmeshed in my creative world in this way."

Um, no. "It was…nice. Do you have a band, Jim?"

"A what?"

"A band," I say, a little louder. Surely his ears are damaged from his profession. Impatience is already settling in, but I must be understanding. It doesn't help that he sounds like he's stoned.

"No, no, nothing like that. I, like, hear it in my head, but I use sticks, or straws, or whatever I can find. I've never played a real set of drums."

Oh my gosh. Where is Bachelor Number One when you need him? I cannot be this understanding!

Jim leans forward and says, "You wanna hear something really, like, real?"

I nod slightly, out of politeness.

"I'm afraid that if I play real drums, it won't sound like it does in my head. I mean, what if it's *different?*" Jim sits back, looking at me as if he has posed the most world-altering question of our lifetime. And he's waiting for my answer.

I stifle a laugh. "Jim, you could be the world's best drummer right now. Undiscovered because you won't actually *play* the drums." I feel ridiculous saying it, but someone should tell him. How sad to play at a passion because you're too afraid to try it for real.

He leans forward and stares at me hard, then tears fall on the edge of the table where he'd been hammering away a minute ago. "Thanks, Laura."

I don't correct him. He cries for a while, and I scoot into the chair next to him and pat his back. He wipes his eyes on a napkin, turns to me, and places his hand on my upper thigh. Uh huh, *upper* thigh.

"Can I come back to your place tonight, Laura? I'm just…like, real upset."

I pat his back, remove his hand from my thigh, and leave. I don't answer, and I'm so glad he didn't bother to remember my name.

Mama picks up on the first ring. "How'd it go, baby? Did I do good?"

"Yes, the first one I'm in love with and have a date with on Saturday, and I can't remember his name. The second one propositioned me."

"Two for two!" She sounds muffled and yells, "Stanley! This is working great!"

I wonder at the "two for two" summation, but whatever. I thank her and promise to drop by Saturday after my date. I forget to tell her to call off her efforts for now, but surely she knows that since I declared love for J.Crew. Oh, I forgot to ask her his name!

I walk by Mrs. Huttle's and glance in the side window. It's after eight, which means she should be on the couch with her light and television on, and she is.

Grabbing for the light switch as I slip in my front door, I pull out J.Crew's card from my pocket.

LARKSPUR

Jason Town,
Citizen of the Republic of Texas,
Let Independence Reign!

That's a nice sentiment. The bottom of the card lists his phone number, but not his job, and it doesn't make a lot of sense to me. I mean, I work at nothing jobs, but if I were to have a business card, I'd rather it say Laun-dro-matio than that I'm a citizen of Texas. Weird sense of state pride there. But who cares?

He has facial hair just lighter than his hair and can send shivers all over me with barely a handholding. Can't wait to call him and hear his voice again. If he wants a Texas flag in the front yard, I can deal with that. I fall asleep later, daydreaming of a house with a giant Texas flag and little J.Crew kids running around the flagpole, holding hands.

At five the next morning I pull on shorts, for the sole reason that I happen to have hairless legs, a shirt, and shoes, and run out the door with extra energy. I'm halfway down the block when the Original Yuppie catches up.

"You in a hurry?" Brant calls.

"It's called running for a reason."

"You just seem faster today." He's keeping pace, looking down at me from my right side. He has on his usual running ensemble, the kind of weatherproof pants and jacket that swish with each step. I don't know why, but I like that sound.

"It's a great day, Brant," I say and turn up the speed, leaving him behind.

Fifteen minutes later we pass, on opposite sides of the street. Red-faced and out of breath, we're both too tired to talk, but I watch him watch me, and after I pass, I turn to see him running one way, still watching me with his head turned.

Poor guy. One day I look like a sick cat and the next I have cute hair, naked hairless legs, and the most flattering pair of shorts eBay ever had for a quarter plus shipping. And that whole "other men want me" energy—any girl knows that's potent stuff.

I accept J.Crew's—Jason's—hand gladly as he offers it to help me from his pickup. Not sure what to wear, I'd gone with a khaki skirt and blue button-down shirt with my favorite sandals—blue with bows. They are so girlie, I love them. With my curveless figure, I gladly take "girlie" anyway I can get it, even if it's only on footwear.

We walk into a school auditorium. I'm surprised at the hundreds of people already there and the flags everywhere—not one of them Texan. I'm a half step behind Jason and speed up to grab the hand he holds out again for me.

He lopsidedly smiles, and my heart flips. I remember the J.Crew kids and the flagpole. We scoot into a wooden bleacher seat just as a guy in a cowboy hat takes the microphone and talks about independence and freedom. I'm not listening really, since Jason is still holding my hand and he keeps looking at me with those amazing brown eyes. I wish we were somewhere else planning our future together. Maybe that's premature, or maybe I'm just a woman of vision.

There's periodic whooping and clapping and fist pumping, a lot like a Texas football game where the fans are into it. You don't have to know what's going on in the game to be supportive, so I whoop and fist-throw, too, and Jason beams and scoots closer. He had called this a rally when he invited me, and I'm only just now wondering what that means.

"I'm so glad you understand," he says into my ear, and alarms are ringing distantly in my head. I ignore them, only thinking that I want him to say something else—anything else—into my ear again.

"Jason, I don't understand at all, but I'm having a great time!" I say to his ear.

He gives me a troubled look, and I try to reassure him by yelling, "Freedom!" with the crowd and flashing him a smile.

After a few minutes, there's a short break and people go around and clap each other on the back and shake hands—like at a church picnic, or at halftime at a high school football game.

Jason doesn't join in but turns to me. "Lark, this is my life, and I need you to understand it."

"So explain it to me! I think your life is a lot of fun!"

"I'm a Citizen of the Republic of Texas. Do you know what that means? Did you listen to anything I said to you the other night?"

How can I say that I was too busy staring at him? I say the first thing that sounds right. "I'm a citizen of Texas, too, Jason! Yea for us!" It comes out kinda wrong.

"*Not* a citizen of Texas. *Never that*. A citizen of the *Republic* of Texas. We're Separatists, Lark."

I lean closer, not wanting anyone to hear me ask what a Separatist is, so I ask in his ear.

He sighs, maybe angry that he has to explain it to me since I thought we were at a fun political pep rally of some sort. "Texas is an independent nation, and we fight peacefully against the occupationalist government of the United States. We accept all religions and races, despite what the media says about us."

"Did you say *occupationalist*?" Oh, is this the group that had a hostage situation a few years back? Uh, yes, I think it is.

"Yes. Is this still 'fun'?" He's studying me, hoping I'll accept his answers.

I can't. No matter how cute he is—and he is *so* cute. Polished, yet still with a rugged look. A little Brad Pitt, when he's scruffy. *So* pretty, but still edgy—however, maybe that's only the whole cult thing he apparently has going on. Despite his prettiness, I can't accept his explanation.

"I'm sorry. I voted for Bush! I'm a conservative Republican, and I *like* being part of the United States, Jason."

"We aren't part of the United States, whether you or anyone else recognize it or not!"

"Okay, in my world we are." I decide to speak calmly and slowly, but I can't think through what I should say that will get me out of this. "I know I'm in your world right now, but if you could drive me back to mine, I'd appreciate it."

This is the wrong thing to say, and Jason stands up and walks off, disappearing amongst the other, far less physically attractive Separatists.

Oh God, help me. Forgive me! I have been lured by lust straight into the Texas underworld. Even the flags are different here.

The crowd seems less like a football bunch now, and I make my exit quickly, wishing I weren't wearing the blue sandals with bows that look great and kill my feet.

I'm two miles from home, which is two miles too far in these shoes. I laugh at the thought of me being a "woman of vision." Such a woman would not be stranded in these shoes, ever. I'm considering calling someone for a ride, but I'm not ready to share the details of this afternoon with anyone yet. I've just stepped out of my sandals when a silver Mercedes slows down, stopping next to me. Boring Brant leans out the window, looking as neat and pressed as he always does.

"Need a ride, Larkspur?" he calls sweetly. He knows I don't like my name.

If I were in any other shoes, my answer would be no. But the asphalt is warm under my feet. Desperate, I force a smile. "Thanks." I hope he doesn't ask why I'm carrying my shoes. I am about to open the passenger door when I see a pretty redhead seated there. I smile at her and slide into the backseat.

She turns around and extends a hand to me, which I shake. "I'm Danica."

"Hi, I'm Lark. Thanks, Brant."

"No problem. What happened to you? Car break down or something?" He's being nice to me because of Danica, but I'm glad anyway.

"Uh, no. Just got…separated…from my ride."

"Oh, I hate it when that happens," Danica says, with what appears to be genuine sympathy.

"Who was your ride?" Brant catches my eye in the rearview mirror.

"No one you know, I'm sure."

"You know, there's a big Texas Independence rally going on back there…gee, that's not where you were, right, Lark?"

I sink lower in my seat.

"Lark?" His tone is innocent and sweet, and so fake. I know it, but Danica doesn't. At the moment I can't stand this man. Or at any other moment. There was a short span of time in high school, though, but no one ever knew. I was hormonally imbalanced then so it didn't count.

"Yes, Brant! That's where I was! I chanted for independence and freedom and even punched the air with my fist. Are you happy? *I* was a Separatist today."

He doesn't say anything, but I can feel his satisfaction the rest of the way to our street. When we get there, he pulls the car over, turns and smiles at me like he's holding back a giant laugh, and hits the automatic unlock button to release me.

Danica says, "I support *all* political views and believe they are separate but equal." She smiles.

Huh? I can picture her at a beauty pageant with the same smile proudly saying, "I support…world peace!"

"Wow, that's, um, nice, Danica. I decided to leave when I remembered they sometimes take hostages to prove their point. But that's just me." I smile insincerely at Brant as I put on my sandals. The thought of Brant with Danica helps me refrain from slamming his perfect, silver door.

Brant is a *bug*, I think, in true second-grader style. He's so great, he probably didn't even notice her beauty pageant looks. And hair! Can't forget the gorgeous, flowing locks of Disney-worthy hair. No, he was entranced at first glance by her endless compassion and tolerance of all "separate but equal" political views. Yeah, that's it!

It's not too hard to figure out why Brant's with the beautiful Danica, but the other way around? I don't know. She could have anyone, I bet. I walk toward my house wondering what in the world she sees in a dope like Brant.

3

I'm relieved to step out of my sandals when I get inside my apartment and remember I told Mama I'd come by today. Taking a few minutes to eat a sandwich and change shoes, I'm out the door again. I peek into Mrs. Huttle's windows as I pass, but I don't see her.

Mama's in the kitchen when I get there, singing loudly while washing dishes by hand. She has a dishwasher, but I've never seen her use it. I think she just likes washing them herself and singing. She stops when she sees me, tosses me a dishtowel, and doesn't bother with a hello.

"How was Hot Date Number One?" she asks.

"More like Disaster Date Number One."

"What happened?" She stops rinsing a plate to study me.

"Do you know what a Texas Separatist is, Mama?"

She thinks for a minute. "No, I don't."

"I didn't either." So I fill her in and we get distracted wondering how many of them there could be in Plains Point. There was a rally of them with hundreds present—so there must be more than we thought.

"I guess I better ask all future men about their politics."

"Yeah, but it's not your fault, Mama." He wasn't exactly keeping it from me. I just zoned out and didn't listen to him. Not that I'm eager to confess that I was blinded by lust. I mean, Mama's cool, but she's still my mother. "If I'd listened closer, I'd have known right away that he wasn't as great as I thought."

"He told you all this ahead of time?"

I take the plate from her so I can dry it. "Yeah. Well, he tried. But he was so *cute*, I didn't listen."

"You said cute didn't matter!"

"It doesn't, but it can be *very* distracting. Ask extra questions of the cute ones."

"Okay, I'll remember that. What about the drummer?"

I laugh at the thought of PseudoDrummer overcoming his phobia of his instrument of choice. "Oh, he has things to work out in his life."

"Never mind, because I have great hopes for Wednesday night's male lineup."

"Ew! Can you please not call it that?" Sounds like Mama's version of a Vegas-style All Male Review.

"Sure, baby. I'll call you about it later in the week. Coming to church tomorrow?"

"Yeah, but not your church." I give her a kiss, and she swats at me playfully as I leave. I tend to keep my visits brief.

It's not easy having a mother like her. She's great and all, but I've learned to keep careful watch over how involved we are. I adore Mama, and if I let her become my best friend, my landlord (she'd love for me to move in), my bank (she's always trying to loan me money), and my matchmaker on top of that, life wouldn't be good.

I could call when money is tight, or become a fixture at her church, or move in to save more money, but I don't do these things. Mama's personality is so *big* that she'd suck me in like a black hole if I got too close. She wouldn't even mean to do it, but it would happen, and I'd be lost forever. So I don't get too close, much as I love her.

My navy Nova sputters a little on the way home, but I don't worry. It's done that for years, and if there were a day to sputter a little at life, this is it.

I can't help but remember how vapid Danica was, and it irritates me that Brant, although being the world's biggest dip, has never seemed to suffer the same shortages of opposite sex companions that I have. From what I can tell, most of them, with the exception of Danica, are as smart as they are pretty. I wonder, not for the first time, what these women can possibly see in him? He's probably not criticizing their hair, like he does mine, but he can't be that great.

He's Brant after all. The same guy who swishes by me, hurling early morning insults, sits on the missions committee at church. In fourth grade he misunderstood the meaning of Inside Out day and wore his underwear over his jeans. Spiderman Underoos, of all things.

He's still that guy, and for some reason, nice girls have always liked him anyway. Not this nice girl. I grit my teeth at the thought of him.

I'm almost to my door when Mrs. Huttle calls my name. "Larkspur!"

"Yes, ma'am?"

"I'm skipping my nap this afternoon." She is wearing her nice yellow housecoat and looks at me expectantly to see if I catch her hidden meaning.

I do. "I'll be glad to mow now then, if it's okay with you."

Mrs. Huttle nods, as if considering this and agreeing, instead of as if she practically suggested it, which we both know she did. Without another word she turns and goes back in her back door, and I wonder what her plans are in place of a nap.

I'm not very good at yard work, but Mrs. Huttle doesn't ever say anything, so I figure she doesn't notice. It's a beautiful afternoon with a breeze and enough clouds to make the sun not too hot. I slather too much sunscreen on my legs, but figure more is better than not enough.

I mow the back first, enjoying the smell of cut grass. I move on to the front, even though the rows I've just mown are about as patchy as the hair behind my left ear. I'm halfway through with the front yard when I notice Brant and Danica standing in his driveway, looking my direction.

Brant is as crisp and put together as ever, and the gorgeous Danica is at his side. A redhead who is so nice, or brainless, she doesn't see him for the dummy he is. He waves at me, but I ignore him, turning the pushmower and walking away, leaving a tall patch between the row I'm mowing and the previous one.

I decide right then that something has to change. Why could I not return that wave? What would be so hard about that? I do not want to war with my neighbor, Mr. Obnoxious, for the rest of my life. I truly don't. I hate the insults, the jabs, the condescension he shows me every time we speak.

I don't know what will change, or how, but I do know when. Right now.

Mid-row of mowing Mrs. Huttle's front lawn, I leave the mower to cough its death as I walk away. My legs feel raw and itchy, and I remind myself to never mow in shorts again, regardless of how nice it is outside or how hairless my legs are. This is what I'm thinking while walking purposefully toward Brant—not about what I need to say. I wish I could plan things like that. Life might be better if I could learn to do that, but no. I simply open my mouth and what comes out is what I have to live with. Like, why tell a potentially hostage-taking Separatist you voted for Bush? That could have used some thought.

As I get close, a car pulls up and Danica jumps in. She gives me a beauty queen, cupped-hand wave, then one to Brant, and she's off. I'm left standing in the exhaust of the red sports car that picked her up.

I cough, stalling.

Brant raises his eyebrows, silently questioning my presence, or maybe my determined but wordless fists-on-hips stance.

"I don't like how things are with us."

"Oh?"

"No. I'm tired of the insults and the nastiness, and I want it to stop. I don't treat anyone else like I treat you, and no one else in my life is as mean to me as you are." I feel dumb but press on. "It doesn't have to be this way, and from now on, it won't." I picture how from now on we will be strangers who will wave civilly and nothing more. I smile because that sounds pretty good.

"I've been thinking the same thing, Lark." He looks down at his feet, and he doesn't seem as sure of himself as usual.

"Great." I hold out my hand for him to shake as an offer of our newfound peace. Instead he takes it and sort of holds it for a second, throwing me so off guard there are even hand tingles. With *Brant!* Utterly unacceptable.

"So let's have dinner later."

"Huh?" I have no idea what just happened, and I've folded my hands across my chest so I'll be ready in case he wants to surprise me again.

"I mean, now that we're friends and all, we could have dinner."

Friends? I didn't say anything about being friends! "That's um, not really what I meant. And what about Danica?"

"Ah, she dumped me. And you came over offering friendship at exactly the right moment, Lark. Thank you."

I did not offer friendship! But he looks so pathetic.

"So, how about I drop by to get you around six?"

Dinner with Boring Brant? Oh, yuck! I have to learn to think before I speak!

"Sure." I smile, but it's a sad attempt, and I hope he doesn't notice my horror at this proposal. He's just been dumped and probably doesn't need to hear that I wasn't offering friendship. What I was thinking was more like, well, nothingness.

"So, friends can joke with each other?"

"Yeah…?" I'm hoping he's going to tell me he's kidding about dinner.

"Great legs, Lark."

I look down. Where my legs should be are Kermit the Frog's legs. Or Oscar the Grouch's legs. Or the legs of any green Muppet, because grass clippings have plastered themselves to my sunscreened legs so completely that I am a freak of a woman with black shorts and green, furry legs. Well, that explains the itching.

"See ya, Brant."

I walk my Muppet-y self across the street to finish the front yard, wondering what to wear to dinner with Brant Stephens. But since he asked while I wore grass clippings must mean I've set the bar pretty low already, and that's good.

My shower takes longer than usual, because it is almost impossible to get all those grass clippings off the shower walls and down the drain. Stubborn things. But it gives me time to decide I won't dress up for a friendly dinner with Brant that I'd rather not be at anyway.

Certainly I won't wear the girlie blue sandals with the bows that look great. The last thing Brant needs is to think that I am wearing uncomfortable shoes for him. And once I ruled out a pair of great looking shoes, I also rule out all skirts and anything nice. Better send the message right up front that I did not find this worth dressing up for. Correction—I do not find *him* worth dressing up for.

So I wear khaki capris with cute bows on the hem, a red shirt with a keyhole neckline, and slip-on, comfortable footwear no one would find alluring.

Brant knocks a few minutes before six. I wasn't expecting that. I guess I thought it would be like when our moms carpooled us in the third grade, and we would go stand by the curb at the appointed time. It didn't seem absurd at all then, and I'd been about to do just that. I take a quick look around my apartment. Buttoned-up Brant won't like it at all, I think, so I swing open the door extra wide.

I'm the first to be surprised, though. He's casually dressed also and looking embarrassed. He holds out a pink tulip, and I recognize it as the late-blooming variety I planted last fall and that are currently blooming in Mrs. Huttle's front yard. I plant her beds so she can see them from her windows—out at the perimeter of the yard instead of where most flowerbeds are, right up next to the house. I recognize this one from a clump near the mailbox.

"Uh, thanks." I haven't decided to call him on his thieving ways, but he confesses.

"Mrs. Huttle insisted. I know you probably recognize it, but I didn't know how to tell her no. She handed me a pair of scissors and pointed me toward the mailbox. She wanted me to take more."

"Mrs. Huttle?" I lean out the door and look to the left. There she is, peering out her back window at us. I wave and grab Brant's arm to pull him inside. "That's weird, but come in so she'll stop looking."

I'm still thinking of how Mrs. Huttle has the wrong idea when I realize Brant is looking around with his mouth open.

"You like?" I ask, enjoying it a little.

My walls are pretty wild. They're all the color of the pale pink tulip I'm putting in water, but one wall is covered in various brightly colored polka dots—as big around as my round laundry basket, which is what I used as a template. Another wall has abstract paisleys and triangles, and still another has vertical stripes over the pink background. The stripes are the same colors used in the polka dots, paisleys, and triangles, and they're a little wavy since I freehanded them. You can get dizzy if you look at that wall too long. I have.

"I think I do like it, Lark." His mouth is still open, but he is nodding in what seems to be genuine admiration. "Does Mrs. Huttle know it looks like this?"

"Probably not. But I asked if I could paint, and she agreed."

"It's *alive*." He tucks his hands in his front pockets and turns slowly, eyes still on the walls. "You know, every wall in my house is white. It came that way, and I never changed it, but lately I've been thinking the place could use some color."

"Every wall is white? And you've lived there how long?"

"Four years. It never bothered me until lately, though." He takes one last look at my "lively" walls, and we walk through the side yard to his car.

I'm not prepared for Mrs. Huttle, though. She's standing on her porch when we pass. "Lark, dear."

"Yes, ma'am?" I've already had one conversation with her today, and that's more than in a normal week.

"I know you look in my windows when you walk by, and you check on me."

I didn't know she knew that. "Yes ma'am, I do."

"That's fine with me, but please don't do that when you have gentlemen callers with you." My face feels hot, and I have only halfway processed that she actually said, "Gentlemen callers."

"Uh, yes, ma'am."

"I would have told you that before now, but it hasn't been necessary."

"No…no, ma'am," I manage, but I could die of humiliation. And I mean, *die*. My heart is racing. The last time I was this embarrassed was when my skirt was tucked into the back of my panties, leaving my entire backside available for scrutiny for a whole hour, on the first day of junior college. Yeah, this ranks up there with that.

Mrs. Huttle smiles at us. "As long as we have an understanding, you two go have fun."

I nod and steal a glance at Brant, whose face is noticeably pink. From amusement, or embarrassment of being labeled my only Gentleman Caller, I don't know. What I do know is that Mrs. Huttle clearly has the wrong idea about Brant and me. We're only having dinner because I didn't think before I proposed nothingness and he had just been dumped by the peace-loving Danica.

I mean, anyone could see we don't like each other.

4

I feel completely out of place in the front seat of Brant's Mercedes. I feel completely out of place being with him at all. He doesn't seem to notice, though, and as he pulls away from the curb he asks if I want to go to the lake.

"Have you been lately?"

I shake my head. Plains Point's one lake isn't much, but it's the only one within a hundred miles. Last time I went it had a few restaurants, and a small wharf with about twenty sailboats moored there.

"On Friday and Saturday nights there's usually a band, and some of the restaurants have gotten pretty good lately."

"Sounds nice." And it does sound nice—not what I thought Brant would like at all. I pictured a boring white-tablecloth sort of place. Instead, he shows up dressed in really nice-fitting jeans and suggests an evening at the lake with a band. Unexpected.

We pick a restaurant with red-and-white-checked, vinyl tablecloths and silverware wrapped in paper towels. Shiny, galvanized pails hold paper menus, and our table overlooks the water. The sailboats rock in their moorings, creaking pleasantly. It's still warm, and the sun tinges everything golden.

"You're smiling," Brant says, and he's right.

Suddenly I remember I haven't gritted my teeth at his presence once yet. But the night is young, so I merely shrug and look at the menu.

"What are you getting?" I ask, just to say something.

"Crab, I think. It's pretty good here. What about you?"

"Ever tried raw oysters?"

He shakes his head and makes a face.

"I think tonight's the night we try raw oysters."

"They look so slimy, though."

"Yeah, I know. Should be fun!"

Brant laughs at me and offers me a roll, which I take. I decide to fill up on bread in case raw oysters don't agree with my empty stomach.

We talk about the sailboats' names we can see, and then the waiter arrives with Brant's crab legs and my enormous platter of iced oysters. The waiter gives some tips on how to eat them, leaves us lemons and Tabasco, and says he'll check on us soon.

I loosen the first one from its shell and hold it out to Brant. He squeezes a lemon over it while I get mine ready and douse it with a few drops of Tabasco.

"Ready?" I can tell he's not, but I count to three and we slurp them down at the same time. It's pretty nasty, really, but it sure makes for fun eating.

"I like that." He looks surprised, and I am too, because I didn't really like it. I can totally do without repeating that experience. After Brant's next one, I can tell he's really into the oysters, and I switch our plates, so I have the crab and he has the oysters.

"Why did you get that if you didn't think you'd like it?"

"I didn't *know* if I'd like it." These things must be explained to Boring Brant, of course, so I add, "And it sounded like fun. I'd never tried it."

"I don't do things that way usually."

I try to look surprised, which of course I am not. "Look at what you've been missing out on. Your new favorite food."

"No kidding. These are wonderful." He slurps another one, and I try to figure out what to do with the crab tools. He shows me, and I decide that Brant's crab legs are much better than slimy oysters.

I sort of get the hang of the crab tools, but a piece of shell flies in Brant's direction and lodges in his hair. We both find this really funny, and he leans forward to let me pick it out. "Did you get it?"

"Um, yeah." I'm laughing because I got a little piece of crab meat in his hair when I took out the shell. "Come back," I instruct.

He leans forward again, and I get the piece of meat. "Sorry." I clack the tool's arms together. "These things are dangerous."

"Good thing no one's at the table behind us; some went that way, too." He's teasing, and I can't help but smile at us and our swapped lakeside dinners. Brant pays the tab, asks for an extra bag of rolls, and we leave.

"You really liked those rolls?" I ask. I didn't think they were that great.

"No, I thought we could go feed the fish. I haven't done that in years, but I just thought of it."

We walk to the very end of the first row of sailboats, and sit. Perfect Lady creaks in her mooring to our left, and on our right sits a newer sailboat named Serendipity. The murky, green lake water is only about four feet below us, and the bright orange sunset is blinding on the water, so we mostly look down at our feet.

I slip off my shoes and put them beside me, and Brant does the same. His feet are really ugly. Surprising, since the rest of him is, well, not. His feet are white and hairy, and the toes look like they're in a traffic jam—not heading all in one direction. We swing our feet in silence before he says, "You have the prettiest feet I've ever seen."

I know he's being sincere, simply because I *do* have gorgeous feet. Christine tells me this all the time when we're painting our toenails, but this is the first time anyone other than her has said so. "Thanks, Brant." I hold them out and am glad that I painted my toenails Copper Coin yesterday. They shimmer as the sun's last rays hit them, as if I'd planned it.

Brant tells me he'll be right back and returns in a few minutes with a windbreaker that I guess he had in the car. He holds it out for me to put on, and it doesn't feel strange to slip into it. He scoots closer, hands me some bread for the fish, and as we drop it into the water, a band starts playing from somewhere behind us on the shore.

Happy fish come to swim beneath us, looking for the next bite we'll throw. Someone in that band has interesting taste in music. And so, surprisingly, does Brant. I'm thoroughly caught off guard when the band plays "La Bamba" and Brant softly sings all of the lyrics in Spanish. And it actually sounds good. I laugh at him and ask why he knows the words to "La Bamba."

"I mean, *no* one knows those words. I don't even think Spanish speaking people know those words."

"I learned them for extra credit in Spanish one year."

"That makes sense." No other answer could have made more sense. That's so Brant. But maybe I don't know who he is anyway. This Brant wears jeans and eats oysters and sings "La Bamba." And he gave me a windbreaker at the exact moment I wished I had one. He pulls me up by the hand when the band starts the Macarena. "Teach me, Lark."

Laughing, I ask him what makes him think I would know.

"Because you're fun. And if anyone knows this, it's you."

"Yeah, I do," I say, and I show him.

When it's almost over, and we're laughing at each other, Brant turns the wrong way and bumps into me with his hip. I trip over my shoes, grab at the dock, but just scrape my hands as I fall to the water below.

The water chills me instantly, since it's April. I go under and picture all the happy, well-fed fish scattering around me. I struggle to come up and laugh at Brant's worried face.

"I'm so sorry, Lark!"

He's looking for something to throw to me, but I start swimming to shore. It's only a few yards before I can touch the bottom. I call this news out to Brant and his face relaxes. He looked about ready to jump in, despite my only being in a couple feet of really cold water, and in no danger at all. I'm shivering by the time I get to the water's edge, and Brant gets there at the same time, having run all the way back for our shoes. He tries to rub warmth back into my arms, but I haven't had time to squeeze out my hair or clothes, so I shrug him off.

"It's okay, Brant, really." And for some reason, it is. But it's funny how concerned he is. It's only a little lake water, and a little cold. Well, a lot cold.

"Here are the keys. Go turn the heat all the way up. I'm going to go see what that souvenir shop has."

It's a sad little shop if I remember correctly, and an odd time to buy souvenirs, but the offer of a heater on high sounds good, and I take the keys. I decide not to get in, though, once I get there. His car is so perfect, and I don't know if the smell of lakewater will ever come out of pristine, beige leather upholstery. Instead I turn the heat on and hover in the door while I continue to squeeze the water out of my pants.

Brant comes back with two oversized, thick towels, one pink

sweatshirt, and one pair of socks with fishing lures embroidered around the ankles. No telling how much all that cost, but I'm too cold to care.

"Why didn't you get in?"

"I wasn't dry, and I didn't want to mess up your car."

"Get in." His tone doesn't leave much room for disagreement, and I slide in. He gets in on the driver's side and hands me things to put on. I notice that he doesn't seem the least bit concerned about his upholstery.

On the way back I lean forward into the glorious heat of the vent, wrap a towel on my head, and wrap the other one around my body.

When he stops in front of Mrs. Huttle's, I shush him from telling me he's sorry again.

"Brant, we should never, never Macarena at the end of a pier again. But tonight was fun anyway. Thanks for dinner." I gather my shoes and purse and the towel that has fallen off my hair and am surprised that he is standing outside my door, having opened it.

The man opened the car door for me. Huh. That has never happened. Ever.

"Uh, thanks." He's holding a hand out, so I take it with my free hand. He takes my load from me, puts an arm around my wet shoulders, and walks me to my door. I'm so rattled by his unexpected show of manners that I fumble with the key.

"You're still cold, here." He takes the key and works the lock. I notice that he is really, really sweaty.

"Are you okay, Brant? Are you sick? Come inside."

"What? Oh, I'm fine. It was a bit hot in the car, that's all." He's wiping the sweat away, and I feel like an idiot. Twenty minutes with the heat on high—of course he's hot!

"Oh, we could have turned the heater down! I'm sorry." It doesn't come across as very sincere, because I'm laughing, too.

"We needed to warm you up." Brant looks at his feet, then back at me. "Are you up for a run tomorrow?" He's backing out of the doorway, hesitant, and the mood has turned awkward.

"Sure." I run a hand through my cold, wet hair and wonder how bad I look after my unexpected swim. Maybe having short hair plastered to my head brings out my eyes. Or, more likely, maybe I'm merely a moron who smells like lakewater. "Um, see you in the morning."

"Good night, Lark." He smiles and turns away, and I can't ever remember seeing him smile so often. And I would remember, because sometime between high school and now, his too-cute perfect pinpoint dimples turned into deep, short parentheses. They call attention to his perfect teeth and act as each smile's own set of exclamation marks, rather than the parentheses they resemble.

Whatever it is, they're really much cuter than the high school version of those dimples. With a few more years they'll be full-blown laugh lines. On Brant! Who knew?

A hot shower washes the lake away and provides enough time to decide that I can never, ever think of Brant in the same way again. He's not boring, predictable, dull, or anything like I'd thought. And I still have his windbreaker. What is it about having a guy's jacket that seems so—personal—anyway? I steal a glance at it on the chair in the corner of my bedroom and immediately go toss it in the back of my closet, to return to him later. It's much too personal to have it hanging around.

5

It's Wednesday morning, and I'm late to class. My professor doesn't seem to notice me slip into my seat. He isn't the only one who's distracted, though. Mama called Sunday after church with a change of plans for tonight and the Man Project. She also changed Friday night's regularly scheduled dating project to Saturday night, just for this week.

I don't think much had been accomplished during her Sunday school class, because the women decided they all knew great singles they could nominate for a "prescreened," invitation-only round of speed-dating. I think Mama's Man Project has inspired others to get involved, and this is the result. But at least the focus is on all of us, and not squarely on me. But how do you speed-date, anyway? She didn't tell me that.

The entire class passes with my mind on tonight, and not on accounting, and the rest of the day isn't much different. By the time I get halfway to Coffee Café, I remember that it's being held at Java, The Hut instead. I speed so I won't be late. Or that's the plan, until the police cruiser that came from nowhere turns on its reds and blues.

I get that awful hot, going-to-throw-up feeling, but pull over without incident. I've only been stopped one other time, and I got that same feeling then, too. And it just gets worse, because it takes the officer forever to approach my side of the car. I don't know what could be taking so long—I mean, technology is instant these days—so I figure he's simply trying to scare me. It's working really, really, well.

Don't throw up, and don't cry.

"License and registration, please, ma'am." His Texan drawl is charming. Sometimes it can be obnoxious, but on this man, it's as genteel and gorgeous as I've already decided he is. His face is angular, sculpted almost. Reminds me of Matthew McConaughey, and let's face it—that is never a bad thing.

I hand over his request, and he asks if I know why he pulled me over. Why do they ask that?

"Yes, sir. You pulled me over because I was speeding. It was 42 mph in a 30."

He smiles, and I was right. He's gorgeous.

"Yes, ma'am. And why are you speeding tonight?"

"My mother is eager to introduce me to dozens of men she and her friends have decided are good-quality Christians, and I went to the wrong coffee shop and needed to hurry up."

Another smile. Or, an expansion of the first one, really. I thought I sounded like a moron, but something tells me that the officer likes me.

"I'm giving you a warning, but you'll probably still be late."

"A warning? Really?" And before I can tell myself to shut up, I ask, "Is it because I'm cute?"

"No, it's not because you're cute." He tips his head to the right. "It's because you're the only honest person I've pulled over today."

"Oh." Disappointment probably shows on my face, because he laughs at me.

"I can't ask you out, you know. Wouldn't be ethical. But I bet your mother would approve of me."

"Oh, I bet she would, too." Not that I care at all, at the moment. This is full-out flirting, and I didn't need Mama for this!

He hands me the warning.

"You know, I'll be at Coffee Café on Saturday night meeting whoever my mother has sent my way." I am bold and brazen. This is no way for a good Southern girl to talk to a police officer, or to anyone else for that matter. I flutter my eyelashes in what I hope to be a subtle gesture of femininity.

He laughs outright at it. "What's your mother's name?"

"My mother...uh, Grace Andrews."

"Have a nice night, ma'am."

I have no idea why I do not know his name, or why he needed to know Mama's name. Maybe he's going to watch out for her. Maybe he's going to go win her approval before passionately pursuing me and sweeping me off my feet.

LARKSPUR

I snort at this, and my runaway imagination of how God will finally provide Mr. Right. I lose sight of the patrol car in my rearview mirror. Officer Gorgeous turned left a few blocks back. *And how quickly I forgot the lesson of Jason and the Separatist Lust! Oops.*

I walk into Java, The Hut late, but Mama grabs me and sits me down in a chair at the end of one of two rows of twelve. The two rows of chairs face one another, and there are giggling women next to me in the chairs to my left. Across from us are twelve empty chairs, and I notice lots of men milling and eyeing the already seated ladies. Most of those men are pretending they're not eyeing us, but we're not fooled.

The girl on my left isn't interested when I introduce myself. She tells me her name is Blanca, but she's busy looking at the men and fluttering her eyelashes in a true gesture of femininity. If I'd managed to learn how to flutter like that, I'd probably have a date with that police officer right now. And I wonder why Blanca is in the seat next to me at all, since she has a Barbie doll body and the eyelash flutter down to an art. Girls like that should be engaged already. Must be something wrong with her.

Everyone else seems to know what's going on, and I figure I missed the part where instructions and helpful tips were given. Great.

Mama rings a gold bell, and the seats in front of us fill with nervous-looking men. The first guy is blond, with pretty blue eyes, and his pale skin keeps flushing red. It's cute, but distracting, and he's so nervous or embarrassed that he looks like he's in physical pain. I don't know how much time goes by—seems like just seconds—when Mama rings the bell again. I watch Blanca to see what she does, but she stays put. The men all shift one seat, and a familiar face sits across from me.

This town must be smaller than I thought. It's Jim, PseudoDrummer.

"Hi, I'm Jim."

I nod, because I know this, and I'm trying to decide if he recognizes me—or my thigh, which he had seemed so interested in getting to know better the last time I saw him.

"You're a quiet one. That's cool. You can just listen."

I roll my eyes as he pulls out two pencils, which he plays on his knee. After what seems like a much, much longer interval of time than with the last guy, Mama finally rings the bell, and I smile my relief as Jim leaves to head to the other end of chairs. Blanca leans over and whispers, "Isn't that one great? I just love musicians."

Yeah, something is wrong with her, all right. I smile brightly and pretend to be looking intently at Mama and her friends, so that I am not drawn into a conversation with Blanca the Barbie.

The men don't seem that great, and I'm glad I only have to spend a few minutes with them. I wonder if they think the same about me and figure they must.

I start to bore myself with the same generic answers. Part-time student, like pasta, etc. So sometime around guy number four I started throwing in something unique, mainly to remind myself that I *am* unique. I like Coke with lemon wedges in the summer, coffee served black in the winter, café mochas year-round, and I only eat Froot Loops dry. Favorite teacher was fourth grade's Mrs. Dahl, who would occasionally stand on her desk and yell at us. But I only managed to entertain myself, I think.

There are only a few more bells to go, and I look down the line to see Brant smiling at me. I wave, surprised I hadn't noticed him before. I remember Mama telling me that Brant's aunt is in her Sunday school class, and that aunt must have vouched for his suitability. He waves back, but the girl seated across from him grabs his hand and holds it possessively as the start bell rings.

At the next break, Mama looks in my direction and says, "Remember, Daters, that you need to choose at least one of your dates. You'll write down the names of your favorite dates at the end. We'll go over names again when we're finished in case you forgot someone's name. And the daters whose slips of paper have matches, your phone number or email address will be given to one another."

I can't imagine wanting anyone I've met tonight to have either of those pieces of information, but I doubt it's likely anyway. I don't think I'll be inspiring many of these guys to write my name down.

Finally, it's the last guy—Brant. We laugh and he leans over and asks if the girl three seats over is still watching him. He's talking about the one who grabbed his hand.

"Nah, Brant. Get over yourself. She has the blond guy's hand in a death grip now."

LARKSPUR

"I'm glad to hear she doesn't think I'm special. She scared me."

Too soon the bell rings and Mama hands out paper and pencils. We're supposed to write our names in one corner and the names of the dates we liked in the middle. But first we all have to say our names, which we do with relief that this is over.

Mama is standing next to me when Brant leans over and whispers, "Do we really have to—?"

"Yes, Daters, you agreed to write at least one name down, and I know that won't be difficult. Remember, the more names you write down, the better a chance you have of getting a match!" She purposefully steps on Brant's toe as she walks by. I don't think Mama agrees with Brant's suitability.

"Mama has amazing ears." I laugh at him, and he tries to wiggle life back into his foot.

I write Brant's name, to meet the requirement, and Mama comes by taking all our papers and telling us it will take just a few minutes to sort out the matches. The Daters wander around Java, The Hut, since we're no longer bound to our rows of chairs. Brant stays close as I order a coffee, probably because the hand-holding girl is still in the room, and he really is afraid of her.

Mama rings the gold bell to get our attention, and three of her Sunday school friends are at her side. They're all beaming at us like the proud mother hens they are.

"Attention! We have had a nice time, and it has gone even better than we expected. All of you have at least one match, and one lucky girl had four!"

Four!? Which lucky girl was dumb enough to write down four of these guys' names in the first place? Well, probably Blanca.

"So you wrote down my name." Brant's smile is set off by those dimple parentheses.

"Uh, well, you seemed the safest," I say, realizing that if everyone had a match, Brant wrote my name down as well.

One of Mama's friends comes up to us, smiling. "We thought this was so sweet. The two of you are the only ones who wrote down just one name." She smiles more broadly and squeals, "And it was a match!"

I didn't expect her high-pitched voice, and I take a step back.

"It must mean something pretty special. We took the liberty of giving you phone numbers *and* email addresses." She hands us our papers, smiles again as if she's my matron of honor, and leaves to deliver more good news.

"Whoa, she really got into this, huh?"

"Yeah, I guess." Brant starts folding his piece of paper into perfect squares, like the architect he is. "So, can I call you?" he asks, and I have no idea how he means this.

"Are you serious?"

"Well, yeah."

"Okay." I guess Brant had a great time the other night, too. I thought so, but it's nice to know it.

"I could use some help painting sometime, if you wouldn't mind."

"Oh." *It's not like you're Blanca. Of course that's all he meant.*

"So, do you mind?"

"No, your white walls are way overdue." I turn down his offer of a ride home, since I have my car, and wave at Mama as I leave.

It's depressing to date twelve men in an hour, and be singled out by just one—not for me, but for my penchant for paint. I must be icky.

I drive home in my ickiness, thinking of Esther. Didn't she prepare herself to be as beautiful as possible for a full year before she met the king? Esther was the opposite of icky.

Me, on the other hand, I forget to shave my legs, fail at flirting with an officer of the peace, and arrive late. And then wonder when no one thinks I'm worth writing down.

I must be more like Esther, I resolve, and I stop at a drugstore on my way home to buy my first ever beauty magazine. I will take a bubble bath and learn all that I am lacking. And I might even shave my legs.

6

I'm up early on Thursday, the night after the unsuccessful speed-dating, and the unsuccessful primping/pity fest I hosted in my bathroom. I counteracted the negativity of reading the beauty magazine with the positive influences of reading the book of Esther. But it was late, and I was tired, and I don't know that my mind really sorted through the messages found in either.

I know I messed up on the part about eyebrows. One look in the mirror verified that, as my left eyebrow has a surprised arch that isn't normally there. I better be more careful with tweezers from now on.

Also, I tried self-tanner and this morning one calf had a white streak where I obviously missed. I tried to fix it, but now I have a darker area where the white spot was and it's outlined in a darker shade of tan. It's so bad, I'm going to have to wear pants until it wears off. So whatever help that beauty magazine was supposed to do for me, it didn't. Maybe I'll reread Esther and try again when my leg returns to all white, and my left eyebrow isn't so surprised.

The phone rings and I grab it, knowing it's Mama. No one else calls this early.

"Hi, Larkspur."

"Hi, Mama." I guess that she's about to ask about last night, so I head her off. "So what do you think about Esther making herself beautiful for a full twelve months before meeting the king? I mean, I tried for two hours last night, and it didn't go well."

"I think you missed the point, and you should reread it. Besides, Esther had seven personal maids who knew what they were doing."

"Oh. Yeah, I missed that part, too."

She surprises me by not talking about the speed-dating fiasco at all and tells me she'll call later because someone is at her door.

I hang up, having no idea why she called in the first place. And with Mama, there's always a reason.

I call Christine to ask how the new StrollerMama is.

"Oh great, Lark. Just great. They knew I was a total fake when I showed up without a kid in my borrowed stroller."

"But how about the class? Weren't you positive and all that?"

"I told them that their children would rise up and call them blessed, and one mom actually laughed and said I obviously didn't have kids yet. In front of everyone! She said her kids rise up and call her 'potty-head' sometimes, but never blessed."

"Sounds like she needed you."

"She needs *something*. Prozac maybe. I'm toning down the 'positive' for now. How's Mama doing with getting you dates?"

"Great! But here's the weird thing. I had dinner the other night with Brant Stephens."

"Ooooh! How was it?"

I'm so surprised that Christine has given Brant an "ooooh" and not an "ew!" that I forget to answer for a second.

"Lark?"

"Oh, yeah. It was great. Um, you think Brant is worth an 'ooooh'?"

"Yummy is hardly something you can say about someone that your friend is dating. Or I would have said that."

"Oh. Huh. But we're not dating." *Yummy?*

"Gotta go. Do you think I should put a doll in the stroller today?"

"No." The bad thing is, I'm pretty sure she asked that question in all seriousness. "Totally *no*, Christine."

I'm still wondering about Christine's unexpected reaction when I see Brant, who decided to run this morning as well. He's in a kelly green whooshing track suit.

Must be my sheer loneliness that makes him so attractive at such an early hour. And it must be my drive to find Mr. Right that has my stomach in knots at the swishing he makes next to me. Certainly it's not any vibe of interest coming from him. He's only interested in my ability to paint his house in wild and funky ways, I needlessly remind myself.

And he's saying something, smiling with those dimples, but I don't hear, because I have just had a fantastic idea. I will paint Brant's house wild and funky and liven it up, if that's all he's interested in, after all. His walls will make my walls look tame, when I'm finished. I'm thinking Rembrandt style tulips, five feet tall in his living room. Ha! Evil scheming complete, I run ahead.

"Lark?"

I look back, and Brant's face is full of confusion.

"Well, do you want to?"

"Do I want to what?" I jog backwards a couple feet in front of him. I really wanted to put on a burst of speed and dramatically exit, and this conversation is getting in the way.

"Do you want to have dinner later?"

How did I miss that the first time around? I fall in a pothole I don't see, because I'm still turned around.

Brant smiles, helps me up, and waits for an answer. I feel ridiculous. The last time he asked me to dinner I had green legs, and this time I fall in a pothole.

"Sure."

"How about the lake again, and I'll pick you up at six?"

"Yeah, but no dancing."

"No dancing," he agrees, and I run off toward my house, not as eager to leave him in my dust as I had been a minute ago.

―――

At 5:45 I have no idea what to wear and no time to spare. I vow to check the classifieds this weekend, to see if I can find just one full-time job to replace my other jobs and crazy schedule. Now that Mama has taken over my social schedule, there's not enough free time for getting ready for those social events. Or for obsessing about what Not-So-Boring Brant really wants, and that itself is taking up way too much time and energy.

I had about convinced myself that he just wanted me to be his painter, but then he asked me to dinner. I decide to hold off on the conclusion that it's a date, since maybe he mentioned paint when I wasn't listening. I must work on listening skills!

I survey my wardrobe and hate that I'm limited by the requirement of pants, thanks to my fake tan smear. I shake the wrinkles out of a pair of denim capris that are just long enough to cover the smear, and a really cute short-sleeved sweater. It's pink, with a bow at the neckline, and my pink sandals look great with it.

Brant knocks at the door exactly at six, and when I open it, he rushes in and shuts it behind him. I didn't expect that, or his worried look, and forget to scoot back. We're standing in a tiny space, way too close. And the distracting charm of a close-up of his dimples makes me not want to step back, so I stay put.

"What's wrong?" I ask, but I'm taken in by his worried expression, and the way he's holding the door shut behind him. An armed and dangerous man could be running across Mrs. Huttle's yard, the way he's acting.

"My mother is here."

"Uh-huh."

"She's talking to Mrs. Huttle, and she's coming to dinner, and I'm sorry for anything she says tonight."

"No problem. Really, you make her sound so great, why don't you go on without me?" I can remember Brant's mom from carpooling, and the profile of her pinched, unsmiling face and blond bun always scared me. I can't imagine she's improved much with age.

"I suggested that, but she insists. She came into town unexpectedly, and I only got her message a short time ago. She said she'd feel awful to mess up our plans and insists that you come."

I'm annoyed to hear that Brant has already suggested that I not come. It's hardly the chivalrous way in which a gentleman caller should treat his future house painter. "Fine, I'll come. But I can't really see your mom at the lake."

"Yeah, me neither, but she doesn't want us to do anything differently than what we had planned."

I raise my left eyebrow, which is already tweezed to such a position anyway, now that I think about it. I lower it and hope Brant hasn't noticed.

"Well, that's what she said."

I follow Brant to where Mrs. Huttle and Mrs. Stephens stand. This non-date could only be worse if Mrs. Huttle comes along. On second thought, maybe it would be better.

I plaster a smile on and greet Mrs. Stephens, who looks much the same as I remember. Her understated turquoise jewelry reminds me that she moved to Santa Fe sometime in the last five years. She wears a raw silk pantsuit in a creamy shade of yellow and silk slingbacks in the same color.

"Larkspuuur, darling, it's nice to see you." She looks me over critically and gives a small nod.

I have a renewed hatred for my name, after hearing her say it only once, with the emphasis on the second syllable. I wave good-bye to Mrs. Huttle, and we walk toward Brant's car.

"I see you haven't given in to the awful flip-flop trend, Larkspuuur."

"Oh, I think they're cute, but it's like having toe wedgies. Why bother?" I knew this was wrong as soon as I said it and start mentally coaxing myself to again learn to think before I speak.

"Toe...*wedgies*? Is that what you said?"

I nod and wish I didn't care about her opinion of me. I never did when I was a kid, and I can't imagine why I would now. I should be older, more self-assured, and less concerned with others' opinions, not more so, right?

Brant flashes me a smile as he opens the front door for his mother. What great dimples that man has! At least he can find the humor in toe wedgies.

We're speeding along when Brant tries one more time to talk his silk-clad mother out of going to the lake.

"You know, there's a nice French restaurant you'd like that got a great review in the paper, Mom."

"No, Brant, we're going to the same place you told me about last week. The one you said you had such a great time at and wanted to go back to. What's the name?"

"I don't even know, Mom. Do you remember, Lark?"

"No, I don't."

I could probably remember the name of the place, but I'm too busy wondering why Brant would be raving to his mother about it in the first place.

Mrs. Stephens turns and glances at me from the front seat. "Brant, I thought you went with Danica." Mrs. Stephens' voice holds a slightly strained quality.

"No, Lark and I went." He catches my eye in the mirror, but I can't understand the meaning of the look he gives me. I can only see one eye and an eyebrow, and whatever it meant, I miss it.

"Danica is such a nice girl. Do you know her, Larkspuuur?"

I see the determined glint in Mrs. Stephens' eye.

"Yes, I did meet her. You're right, she's lovely," I say, and Mrs. Stephens nods at my answer and turns around. *Dumb as all get-out, but lovely, just the same.*

I breathe a sigh of relief that I have survived round one, and hope that round two won't start until after salad.

I swallow a laugh at the sign when we pull into the parking lot. It simply reads: *Lake Eats*. Nothing could be more plain than that. It could as easily say, *No silk pantsuits allowed* in the window.

After a few minutes of menu browsing, Mrs. Stephens asks Brant what is good here. Her question is loaded with the implication that she doesn't believe anything could be good here.

I watch over my menu to see her grimace as Brant tells her that the raw oysters are delicious, and he's having them again. She doesn't answer and orders the salmon. I order the fried catfish with hushpuppies, because I'm such a classy sort of gal.

I try to stay out of the conversation, as Mrs. Stephens talks about the latest project of Santa Fe's Local Artist Association. From what I gather, she's not an artist but is so knowledgeable about art and fundraising that she's an active member of everything they do. I'm bored stiff but thankful she's not talking to me. I can get away with the occasional nod.

I laugh at my plate when it arrives. The catfish is fried in cornmeal to a yellow brown, almost the same color as the hushpuppies. I hadn't expected the fish to still have its whiskers. It's more than a little gross looking.

Brant laughs too and leans across the table to look at it more closely.

His mother waits until the waiter leaves and asks, "Are you a catfish fan, Larkspuuur?"

LARKSPUR

"No, not really. I just ordered it in the interest of authenticity." I drop my napkin in my lap and see that she's waiting to see what that comment could possibly have meant. "I mean, I had the crab legs last time, and we're here at this beautiful lake watching the sunset, and there's an entire menu of seafood that surely didn't come from that Texas lake." I point to her salmon and to Brant's oysters. "This was the only thing I thought might have come from there, and that was reason enough for me."

"I daresay that is not how most people order their meals, Larkspuuur." The disapproval I hear in her voice thrills me. Sometime in the last 10 minutes I decided I didn't want this woman's approval after all.

"I daresay not," Brant adds, then prays over our meal without preface. While he prays, I wonder if his "I daresay not" was an attempt at making fun of his mother, but I can't decide.

Mrs. Stephens takes delicate bites of her salmon, which I don't think she cares for, then launches into a line of questioning about Mama.

I actually remember to think before I speak, opt for all-out truth, and relish the shock I am about to cause. "If you really want to know, her new project is finding me a husband. And if you remember, Mama doesn't do *anything* halfway. She screens all these men—I have no idea where she meets them—and sets me up on endless dates with the ones she approves. She calls it 'weeding out the bad ones.' I wasn't sure about the idea at first, but it's actually very helpful."

Mrs. Stephens' lips are parted a bit, and I smile. I think we can safely declare that Round Two goes to Larkspuuur.

Brant puts his oyster shell down. "I didn't know any of this."

"I guess it never came up, Brant."

"And what does your mother think of Brant, Larkspuuur?" Mrs. Stephens is totally focused on me now, salmon forgotten.

"About Brant? I never asked her. But now that you mention it, I don't think she likes you much, do you?" I ask Brant. "I mean, she stepped on your foot on purpose the other night. That can't be good."

"Well, I applaud your willingness to include your mother in your personal life. I think that's a suitable show of respect."

She's clearly relieved that Mama doesn't like Brant, and I hope she's going to back off now.

"Brant shares that view and promised me years ago that anyone he's serious about would have to first gain my approval, didn't you, Brant?"

"I did promise that," Brant says slowly, stacking empty oyster shells one on top of another.

I watch, fascinated that even while he eats, he's an architect—assembling and creating, weaving stability into a structure of shells.

"Such a nice example of a son living out the commandment to 'Honor Thy Mother.'" She pats his knee and looks back and forth from him to me.

I hope the wave of nausea she just gave me goes away soon.

"So, if your mother doesn't care for Brant, and I can't imagine *why* that would be, and Brant isn't serious about you, Larkspuuur, because I would have heard about it by now, why in the world have you two come to this restaurant twice in one week together? I gather it's not for the food." She eyes her dry salmon.

I didn't see that one coming at all, and my face feels hot. I twist my napkin into a knot in my lap and look at Brant, who appears as caught off guard as I am.

Fortunately, he clears his throat and answers her so I don't have to.

"Mother, I like Lark. I like this place, I like the food, and I like eating the food at this place, with Lark." It's a rhythmic, simple, almost Dr. Seuss sort of answer.

Mrs. Stephens' mouth hangs open, and so does mine.

"If you'll excuse me for a minute." Brant leaves in the direction of the restroom, confident he has silenced his mother.

She turns her gaze on me, and I debate making a run for the ladies' room. I figure she can follow, so I give a small smile and wait. I wonder if now is a good time to tell her to quit calling me "Larkspuuur."

"He said he likes you." It's an accusation that can't be missed.

At that moment, Brant's carefully constructed tower of oyster shells gives way, and they clatter to the plate. Some fall to the vinyl tablecloth, and a couple keep on going until they hit the floor. One industrious shell rolls into the aisle to my left before stopping.

"Oh, Mrs. Stephens, he also said he liked the food, too, and that can't be true," I offer. Then, out of desperation, I add a hollow laugh that comes out a little too loudly.

She narrows her eyes, folds her elegant hands in front of her, and waits for me to say something else. She's good, this lady.

"The truth is that Brant likes the way my apartment is painted and he'd like me to paint his house. He won't tell you that's the only reason he's hanging out with me, but it's true. So don't worry. When he says he likes me, he means he likes what I can do for his walls. That's it."

A waiter walks by and steps on the runaway oyster shell. It skids under a table across the aisle.

"Oh. Well, I can't imagine why he didn't ask me. I could have any number of my artist friends come do a custom job—whatever he wants." She looks hurt but relieved.

When Brant returns, he suggests a walk on the wharf, but Mrs. Stephens declines. I echo her sentiment, saying I have to work later. I wish I hadn't because then Mrs. Stephens wants to know about my jobs and becomes visibly repulsed at the description of my blue-collar life and pulling a night shift at the Laun-dro-matio. She's clearly praising God Almighty that I've already told her that her son doesn't like me, and I'm glad of it as well. Otherwise she'd still be in attack mode.

Brant is starting the ignition when he belatedly says, "You know, Lark, I admire that about you."

Mrs. Stephens' head jerks around so fast that her bun loosens.

"Admire what?" I ask.

"Admire that you do whatever jobs need to be done, and you never act like they're beneath you."

Mrs. Stephens gives an almost inaudible grunt, and I don't have to wonder what that meant.

"They're not...beneath me. But I have thought about consolidating my schedule to get one job that would pay the same as the others. I just haven't found one yet. But that change won't be because I'm too good to work at the Laun-dro-matio, or the bookstore, and I like working for Mrs. Huttle. It'll be because I'm working somewhere else."

I can tell that Mrs. Stephens has recovered somewhat, although Brant got a glare when he dared voice admiration.

"Larkspuuur, what would you like to *do* with your life?" Her question probes at my apparent lack of ambition. Can't blame her for that one, but I'm not about to tell her I'm a closet case of a wannabe number cruncher.

"Oh, I take classes—mainly in accounting and business. I'm not sure what I'm going to do with that knowledge one day, but each semester I pray over which classes to take, and those are the ones I go with. It's an unusual system, but it's worked so far."

"And when do you graduate?"

"I don't think I will. I mean, nothing is really falling into a degree plan. I'm not going to school for the piece of paper that proves I did my time. I'll be done whenever I'm done."

"I didn't know that, Lark," Brant says.

For the second time tonight I answer, "I guess it never came up."

"So, how many credit hours do you have, anyway?"

I tell him, and he says, "Are you sure?"

"Yeah. Why?"

"That's almost as many as I have, and I have my masters. How did you do that going part-time?"

"I started getting credit hours in high school, did a lot of Internet courses, tested out of some classes, went year-round. That sort of thing. I guess it adds up."

"So you *could* have a degree, and you don't," Mrs. Stephens summarizes with a frown.

"I guess so."

"Seems rather unorganized."

I smile at her audacity. *Did you hear that, God? Mrs. Stephens thinks we're going about this all wrong and could be better organized. Big talk from a woman wearing silk to Lake Eats.*

7

Friday morning my email is full of free shipping offers from online stores, cheesy forwarded messages from various people, and one intriguing message from andiloveher@msn. I click on it, and it reads:

> Lark, thanks for last night, and for being nice to my mother. If you're not busy Saturday morning, do you want to go pick out paint? I'll probably choose 10 kinds of beige if you don't come with me, so please say yes.
> Brant

I reply:

> Yes, but I want to see your walls before we go buy their new outfits. And why andiloveher?
> Lark

That has to be the most ridiculous, unprofessional sounding email address I've ever heard, and for it to be Brant's—even more strange.

I'm just closing my laptop when Mama calls.

"Larkspur, what have you been doing?"

Her tone suggests I've been up to something, but I can't imagine what. What have I done to deserve that question in that tone? I've been pretty good.

"Uh, I just checked email." I'm like a 10-year-old, stalling so I can figure out how best to stay out of the maternal line of fire.

"No, I mean, you've been getting speeding tickets and flirting with police officers, haven't you?" I can tell she's trying to sound stern, but she's teasing. I missed that before.

"It was a warning, not a ticket. And you have spies all over this town, don't you, Mama?"

"And you have interested men all over this town, Lark…namely one Officer Tom Trace."

"Ooh, nice name. I've just been thinking of him as Officer Gorgeous. So tell me how you know what you know. Now!"

"The other day when we were talking and someone was at the door—well, that was Officer Trace. Great name for a police officer, now that I say it like that. Anyway, he came to win my approval and ask for your name and phone number."

Exactly as I'd stupidly fantasized! Wow, that *never* happens! "You gave it to him, right? Tell me you gave it to him!"

"Yes, I gave it to him, so tell me how it goes whenever you go out, honey. Tonight you have to be at Coffee Café at seven. There will be an artist coming to see you then, and a nurse at 7:30."

"Yes, ma'am. Thanks, Mama."

"Only doing what any mother would do for her baby if she had the time, love, and immense talent for interpersonal relationships that I do."

"I know, Mama."

I don't add that I am probably in the minority of young women who welcome their mother's input into their dating lives, too. But it makes sense. Like she said, she has the time, willingness, and ability to organize my personal life in a way I'd never be able to. I guess I could tell her to stay out of it, and keep on the way I was, but I wasn't getting anywhere. Besides, I just don't have that much pride. I need all the Mama Help I can get, as long as she's offering it.

My cell phone rings as I'm hanging up with Mama. "Hello?"

"And I love her! What do those words mean to you?"

For a first-ever phone call from Brant, these are interesting first words, I'll give him that. Totally knocks the air out of me.

"Lark…?"

"Uh, hi Brant. I'm not good at riddles."

"That's the best Beatles song ever, and it's underappreciated. My email address seeks to correct that injustice."

LARKSPUR

"Okay, then. I will adequately appreciate that song from now on."

"Great. Want to come over about nine tomorrow and look at my white walls?"

"I'll be there."

"And Lark?"

"Yeah?"

"Thanks. I-I really appreciate you doing this for me."

I can tell that he does. Maybe I won't go all crazy on his walls after all.

"No problem. Bye."

"Good-bye."

~

Friday afternoon I'm sitting on my regular table in the Laun-dro-matio. It's just Christine and me, no customers, painting our toenails Electrocution Pink. Which bothers me, because surely there's nothing pink about electrocutions, but the color is pretty anyway. Shocking, but pretty.

"Pretty. The next one I want to try is Ooh La La."

"Is it pink?"

"Mmm-hmm. Shimmery, pearly pink." Christine swings her feet off the edge of the folding table, to dry her toenails. "I was thinking you should try a Waterbra."

"A what? No, never mind, don't answer. No."

"Why not? I hear they're great."

I doubt that Christine has heard any such thing but don't say so. "Do you remember when you were a kid and you drank a whole lot of water and then jumped up and down just to hear it slosh in your stomach?"

She nods.

"I bet it does that. Gross."

"No! I'm sure they don't slosh. They're too expensive to have gross sound effects, I think."

"Then no for a thousand other reasons. I'll stick to my 12-year-old boy body, thanks."

"Your standards are way too high."

I look at Christine, incredulous. "*Surely* not. Breasts are not too much to ask for on a 26-year-old woman. That's not unreasonable."

"Seriously, Lark. Look at all the couples we know at church who got married or engaged in the last year or two."

"Okay, that would be Randy and Jackie, Trina and what's-his-name, and Celeste and Trina's ex-boyfriend."

"Right. And who of those actually looks like a celebrity?"

"No problem. Celeste."

"Okay, you can't count her."

"That's not fair!"

"No, really, you can't." And Christine gives me a look, but I don't know what it means.

"Why not? You can't tell me that my standards are too high, ask me to name the recently marrieds that look like supermodels, and then make an exception when there really *is* one!"

"Fine." Christine leans over, even though it's only the two of us. "She's had 'work' done. So you can't count her."

"Nooo! Celeste?"

"Yes, but I don't want to talk about it."

"You have to tell me what she's had done!"

"No, I *don't*. And you will not lure me into ugly gossip, Lark."

"Oh shut up! You started it!" I laugh at her.

But I make an exaggerated pucker, in my best Angelina Jolie impersonation, and Christine nods. Lips? Hmm. Well, that's a ridiculous body part to obsess over and go to such lengths as surgery for. I mean, how totally shallow. I'm so glad Christine told me. Boobs, well, anyone knows that's different. Not that I'd go for surgery, even if I could afford it. At least I don't *think* I would.

"So, my point was that your standards are too high. No one else has this idealized, perfect body thing and they're all getting married and engaged right and left. To nice guys. So what's so special about you, that you have to have a smokin' hot bod?"

I so object to those last three words, I cannot even respond.

"Seriously. You have a cute little figure, and the sight of you isn't exactly sending anyone running in the opposite direction."

LARKSPUR

"Right." I decide to agree with her, in the hopes she will never use that "smokin' " phrase again. "Maybe I'm just really shallow, and expect that anyone I end up with will be as well."

"Maybe." She nods sagely. "Maybe you are shallow. You do seem to be especially taken in by a guy's looks, after all. It makes sense you'd assume they're the same way."

I open my mouth to protest, because I hate it that she probably hit on an ugly truth about me. My phone rings, and it echoes through the empty room, the sound bouncing off the linoleum and metal appliances.

"Is this Lark?"

I know right away who it is, but try not to sound like I know. Christine stops to watch my end of the conversation.

"Yes…?" I feign aloofness but kick my Electrocution Pink toenails up in the air in excitement.

"This is Tom, and I have managed to get your mother's approval to call you…we met the other day when you were in a hurry?"

"Oh, yes. Mama mentioned that she met you. Congratulations on winning her over." I make it sound like it's a hard thing to do, but Mama probably took one look at him and his badge and handed over my phone number without asking him anything.

"I was calling to see if you'd go to a picnic with me on Sunday afternoon?"

A picnic? Sounds a little cozy for a first date. "Sure, do you want me to bring anything?" I say, remembering that "cozy" might be rather nice with Officer Gorgeous.

"No, I'll take care of it. I have to set up the tables, though, and well, I hate to ask you to meet me there…but would you mind?"

"Uh, no. I don't mind, but why do we need tables?"

Christine leans close to me, to try to hear Tom's end of the conversation as well.

"Oh! I didn't say that this is a church picnic. I'm sorry. First Lutheran is on Second Street, and I got volunteered to be there early to set up. But it starts at 12:30."

"I'll meet you there, then." Suddenly, not so cozy at all, but he gets points for not thinking I'd mind going to a church picnic on a first date.

That's probably not the first choice of most guys, and I like his originality. "Bye."

Christine waits until I hang up before demanding details. I give her the few that she didn't hear for herself, and she finishes my toenails while I talk. She's much better at it than I am, and when I'm messy it irritates her.

"You know, I think this dating thing is okay and all for you. But I've decided to not date, not look, and just wait."

"Really?" This is a big surprise, since Christine is constantly "looking." "Didn't you say Brant was 'yummy'?" I can't help but ask.

"I formed that opinion before, in my 'looking' phase."

"Oh, right."

"Now I'm doing that totally holy approach where I wait for God to hand deliver The One into my life."

"Isn't that what I was doing before?"

"No." Christine scoots closer on the table and motions for me to move my foot to the left. "You just had a dating drought. Nothing holy about that. There are actually books on what I'm doing." She looks especially smug about this.

"Like there aren't a bazillion more books on dating droughts. So when did you start?"

"Today."

This is so funny, because Christine set up her senior prom date at the end of her sophomore year, so she wouldn't have to worry about potentially not having one. I can't imagine her sitting back calmly and waiting for The One to come knocking on her door. Not Christine.

"Aren't you sort of tempted to think that God is going to be so moved by your 'holy' sacrifice, that He'll deliver The One more quickly than you would have found him otherwise?"

"That's an ugly thing to say!" Christine sticks her bottom lip out a little. "You're asking if I'm trying to *manipulate* God?"

"Yeah, I guess, I mean, I'm sure people take that approach and do it well and all. Are you one of them?"

"I'll think about it." She looks annoyed, and I wasn't trying to bug her, but I accidentally hit a nerve. As she's leaving, Christine asks me to be her "StrollerMama workout guinea pig."

"Your *what?!*" And could there be anything that sounds worse than that? And why do I feel like I'm going to have to say yes?

"You know. You can come with me and I'll try new stuff on you first."

I sigh and say yes, since I accused her of manipulating the Almighty, but I so don't like the sound of this. I have got to think before I speak!

"Will I at least have a stroller?"

"Maybe. I'll call you."

"Great. Bye."

Christine leaves, flip-flops in hand, since she doesn't mind toe wedgies and doesn't want to smear her Electrocution Pink.

When she's gone, I call Mama to tease her. "You know, Mama, you've really changed my social life. Did you know that just between Wednesday and Sunday I will have had 16 dates, and three other pseudo-dates? I mean, no dating service could come close to that!"

"Sixteen? Twelve on Wednesday—speed-dating style, and two on Friday, and I guess Tom is the other date?"

"Yeah, that's pretty good for your being new at this."

"What's a pseudo-date?"

"An outing with someone who isn't a friend and isn't a date." It's a definition Christine and I came up with years ago. I've had cause to use it far more often lately than the definition of "date."

"And you've had three of these?"

"No, two, but I have another one coming up."

"With the same person?"

"Yeah."

"Doesn't sound very 'pseudo' to me, baby. Who is it?"

"Oh...well, that's not what I called to talk to you about. I'll let you know how Sunday goes with Tom. He's taking me to a church picnic."

"Ooh! Extra points for that!"

"That's what *I* thought! Bye, Mama!"

⁓

Saturday morning I am not even tempted to run. It's overcast and drizzly, and the covers snuggle me deeper into their warmth. It's the only sort of morning that I sleep in.

By the time I get up, I don't have long to shower and dress before meeting Brant at nine. I grab a double-orange popsicle as I leave and eat the right half first. I always eat the right half of the popsicle first and then separate the halves and their sticks only when necessary. I don't know why, but it seems more fun this way.

I'm almost to the popsicle demarcation point when Brant opens the door. He's in shorts, which he hardly ever wears, but totally should more often.

"Hi, is that breakfast?"

I nod.

"Come in. Orange is my favorite." He steps aside to let me in.

"Really? Here." I split the two and hand him the left side. Brant looks surprised but takes it and eats it anyway.

His house is sad looking. I mean, the black leather furniture is nice, but it's black leather furniture in a living room with white walls. And no color anywhere. I didn't figure Brant for the contemporary type, but he is. I'm a little disappointed. Lots of white and black and metal and one trapezoid-shaped glass-top coffee table. No kidding, *trapezoidal* furniture. Big, big ick for that.

"It's pretty cold in here."

"Cold?" He has no idea I don't mean the temperature, so I explain.

"Yeah. *Cold.* Metal and glass and no color and a lot of hard edges. That's not you, is it?"

"No, that's why you're here. Because this isn't anywhere I ever want to be. I guess 'cold' does make sense." He shows me the dining room, which is empty except for another glass-top table and silver, modern-looking chairs. Down the hallway, the bedroom doors are open. He uses one for his office, and it has a desk and a rug in a puke-y green color.

No points for using color if the only one you select is puke-y green. The other bedroom is filled with nice furniture—all of it too modern for my taste—and no color. Even the bedspread and pillows are white. It feels weird to be looking at his bedroom, so I backtrack down the hall.

"Okay. You know, we can start with your walls, but really, I don't think it'll be enough."

"What do you mean?"

"Well, um, there isn't anything *soft* in the whole place! Just adding color will help, but all those hard, cold edges make you feel like you're in some sort of institution."

"Yeah, I know."

I'm relieved to leave the place behind as we head to Home Depot. "I'm not a designer or an artist, Brant. Maybe you need a professional." I don't mean to be rude to him, but now that I've seen the place, I think I'm in way over my head. "You know, your mother said she could have an artist of your choice come help you with this."

"Where do you think I got all that furniture?"

"Oh. *Really?* Doesn't seem like her style."

"No, but it's her version of what a bachelor architect's style should be, and I never told her I didn't really like it that much. Some of it I do like, but now that every room is filled with it, well, it's too much."

"No kidding." I ask him what colors he likes, and we head into Home Depot with a mission to paint away the influence of his mother.

The paint department of Home Depot is a wondrous place. I'd forgotten that Bill, from our Sunday school class, works there, and he and Brant start talking about church stuff. I'm eager to see the pretty paint chips and faux finish display, and I wander off.

When Brant catches up to me, I'm on the next aisle deep into a duel with a seven-year-old. His parents were boring him stiff, and he held up a free wooden stir stick and asked if I wanted to fight. I did, and we've been wielding them like swords for a while now.

The kid's name is Max, and we haven't said much more than that. The *thwack, thwack, thwack* of our dueling paint sticks is really satisfying, though, and we've been hitting harder just to make the sound carry further.

Brant stands behind me for a moment, watching. I'm wondering how he feels about my maturity level matching this seven-year-old's when Max's parents call him from the end of the aisle. He gives one last *thwack*, which hits me square on the wrist, and he leaves with his hands over his head in a celebration of victory.

"Having fun?"

"Yep. That was Max. He doesn't talk much."

Brant nods, and I can tell he hasn't been bothered by my seven-year-old maturity level, after all. "Where should we start?"

I massage my wrist and steer us toward the pretty paint chip section, which I still haven't adequately admired.

Brant picks up almost every single color, and then applies the most time-consuming decision-making process ever in order to whittle it down to one shade. So there are nine bazillion reds, and I think, *Great. Brant likes red. This will be easy.* But then he takes forever to decide which shade of red, and I will not even go on about how he does that.

I will say that there's a lot of thoughtful eye closing and opening, and holding paint chips at arm's length. And since there's not another bored seven-year-old around to play with, I stand there and yawn. When I realize he's going to have a huge number of paint cans, I get one of those flat-wheeled carts with the orange metal handles. I sit on it like it's a giant metal skateboard, and wait as the cart around me fills up as one of Bill's coworkers mix Brant's paint choices.

Brant grunts a few times, asks my opinion a couple of times, and takes longer than I would have thought possible. I snort when 15 minutes of narrowing down the yellows actually yields the choice "Yummy Yellow." Can't wait to tell Christine that one!

But it's a whole house of white, and these decisions are way overdue, so I sit there feigning patience I do not feel. I'm eye-level with his very hairy legs, and I entertain myself by studying them. Exceptional legs, and what is it about a guy with really hairy legs, anyway? It's either really nice, like now, or it's nasty-gross.

And when it's really nice, like right at this moment, it's very, very *male*, I decide. Like a mustache, except I usually don't like those.

I feel feminine simply by proximity. Just by being close to such male, hairy legs, I feel as girly as I do in my blue sandals.

I decide I might be crossing some invisible lust-line by studying Brant's legs like this, so I wander off and return with ugly canvas paint masks from a bin at the end of the aisle. Pretending I am a surgeon, I put one on, and slip the other on Brant while he holds out two strips of blue paint chips at arm's length. He leans over, never taking his eyes off the

LARKSPUR

paint chips, and I adjust it so that it fits over his nose and mouth as it should.

Then we carry on as before, me studying his legs, and he studying blues, while wearing masks. I find it more entertaining to do this while masked, and Brant doesn't seem to mind. And, I realize, I've just made studying his hairy legs way more medical than lust-y. Yea for me!

"Brant, Lark, y'all still doing okay?" It's Bill, and I'm so bored that a conversation with him is not nearly as boring as I thought an hour and a half ago.

I invite him to sit with me on the big skateboard, and we talk about paint. I listen with genuine interest as he describes the best times to use latex or oil based paints. He goes to help someone else, and I find it greatly amusing that he never asked why Brant and I were wearing paint masks the whole time. People must do it all the time, after the allure of the paint aisle wears off and boredom sets in.

"Are you ready?" Brant finally asks.

Ha! Am I *ready?* I think he even says it with a straight face, though I can't tell, of course, because of the mask.

"Yes," I answer demurely. He can't see me grinning at him.

And he pushes the cart, while I sit amongst the paint cans and other supplies he picked up. I tell him all about my favorite childhood book, *Mabel and the Rainbow*. The first pages have black and white, simple illustrations of Mabel's house. There isn't any color at all. The furniture, the walls, the rug, everything is bright white. And then Mabel lets in a rainbow, and by the end of the book everything in every room is a brilliant, beautiful color, and the whole house looks amazing. Just because she let the rainbow in. It was a wonderful decision, and Mabel lives happily ever after, in full color instead of boring black and white. "The End," I finish.

"Are you my rainbow?"

"Huh?" We reach the cashier, at last, and I hurriedly put paint cans on the counter for her to scan. "How corny! *This* is your rainbow, Brant." I point to all the cans. "I'm just along for the ride." I take off his mask, which I think he forgot he still had on, and mine, and hand them to the cashier.

KELSEY KILGORE

Two hours later we're back at his house with takeout hamburgers, too much paint for just one house, and no idea where to start.

"The bedroom?"

And that, folks, was the voice of his Y chromosome. That question was as uniquely male as his hairy legs. "How about the room you spend the most time in…which would be this one?" I suggest, looking around the living room.

"Sure." We face each other, cross-legged on the floor with hamburgers. Brant doesn't know what color he wants, so I ask him what he likes.

"What I like?"

"Sure, you insisted on paint in so many colors, we need to narrow it down. Tell me anything—it could be food or music, or whatever comes to mind."

He bites his hamburger and thinks while he chews. "Sunsets, water, clouds, trees, orange popsicles—all popsicles except red."

"Me too, those taste like cough syrup. So, a nature lover, and a popsicle admirer."

"Yeah, I guess so."

We decide on Yummy Yellow for most of the walls, and an orange popsicle-colored semicircle on one wall. It could be popsicle-ish or abstractly sunset-ish, but it definitely won't be white. And it definitely won't be to his mother's liking, but I don't say so.

Brant tapes off the woodwork with the precision I've already come to expect from him. I drape everything in clear, plastic dropcloths. I realize we didn't get primer, but Brant says the walls are already primed.

"What do you mean, 'already primed'?"

"The previous owners had the whole house primed, then didn't pick paint colors because they had to put the house up for sale unexpectedly."

"Having primed white walls is even sadder than having plain white walls, Brant. I mean, do you have to redo it after so long?"

"I don't know. It should be okay."

So we start painting with yellow, and I can't help but think how pathetic it is to have had walls just waiting to be livened up with color, and to instead remain neglected for so long.

I'm dancing to the Beatles, and halfway through the second coat of Yummy Yellow when Brant asks, "How is, uh, how is the thing with your mom going?"

He's so uncomfortable asking, I wonder why he bothered at all. "Great. She's a natural at it. I have two dates later and one tomorrow!"

"Later, as in today?"

"Yeah, it's usually Friday night, but this week we changed it to Saturday."

He looks worried, so I add that I have a few more hours before I need to leave, and this room will be done by then. He doesn't seem to believe me, but a couple hours later the room is done, and I'm washing brushes and rollers in the kitchen sink.

When I finish, I return to the living room where Brant is standing in the middle. His white T-shirt has a yellow streak, and so does one muscled, hairy leg. The dropcloths are wadded into a ball, and he's surveying the change. It's dramatically different, but he looks disappointed.

"Not what you wanted?"

He turns to me. "No, it's just what you said—about the color not being enough."

"Oh, yeah. Well, start with some pillows to brighten up that black couch, and maybe even a rug. If you're really feeling crazy, you could put a vase of flowers somewhere."

"A vase of *flowers*?"

"Don't worry—it won't affect your testosterone level at all. And don't ever buy anything white or black or glass or silver again. You have enough of that stuff in here for the whole neighborhood. Think color and soft."

"Soft," he says, thoughtfully, looking at me. This word is bothering him for some reason.

"See ya!" I turn back in the doorway, and Brant is still pondering the meaning of the word *soft*. Must be hard for an architect to do that. "I'm free tomorrow after three, if you want me to come back," I offer.

"You're not *busy*?"

"No, I'm free after three if you want me to come back," I repeat, slower this time. Smart man has succumbed to paint fumes, apparently. Maybe it would have been better to mask him here when there were actual fumes, instead of at the store.

"That would be great, Lark. Thanks."

I'm tired and dirty, but I hurry across the street anyway. My role as paint mentor is over, and now it's time to give a little thought to men. Let the fun begin!

8

I'm sitting at Coffee Café, on time, and sipping a café mocha when Mama calls. "Lark, baby, your first one just called and he won't be there."

"Okay."

"He's the nurse, and he got called in to cover someone's shift. He asked me if I could reschedule him."

"No problem. I'll take a walk until I meet the artist. What's his name?"

"Uh, Matthew? Mark? Maybe Luke."

"Yeah, thanks for that, Mama."

I go for a walk, admiring the flowers in the pots outside the businesses, awaiting a man whose mother probably named him after one of the books of the Gospel.

Turns out his name is John, and he's *so* nice, but he won't really look at me. He's cute in a scruffy, artistic way, with sandy, messed-up hair and bright green eyes.

The already stilted conversation stalls out completely, and he turns to me and says, "Lark, here's what happened. I was very excited to meet you because I'm trying to move on with my life."

Red flags go up in my mind at the phrase "trying to move on with my life."

"Then my ex-girlfriend called me today and asked me to visit her next weekend, and I'm really hoping we're going to get back together. She just moved to Austin, and I'd like to go to school there anyway."

"Uh huh." I can't believe that one guy stood me up and the other showed up to talk about his ex-girlfriend.

"So I've been planning to move there anyway, and now it can't happen soon enough."

"Okay, no problem."

"I didn't know if it would be worse to come here when my heart is still with her, or if it would be worse to back out of a commitment I made to your mother."

So I totally let him off the hook and our conversation gets much friendlier, and he *gives me his job!* Well, sort of. He's the Coordinator for Classes at the Arts Center, and he has been looking for a replacement to suggest at the same time he gives his notice. Now he really needs one since he's planning to move closer to his ex-girlfriend, and he thinks I'd be great!

It must have been the yellow paint under my fingernails. That or God, you know. He tells me all about the job, which sounds great, and all I have to do is impress the boss at an interview. According to John, that's not a problem and to plan on starting in two weeks since that's when he's hoping to move. I gladly give him my phone number as we part, and he looks just as pleased.

Thank You, Jesus, for John and his job! I get in my car, praying blessings over his potential reconciliation with his girlfriend and then wonder if I'm only doing that in the name of future job security. Deciding I am, I repent of my selfish prayer, but then hum "Love Me Do" all the way home.

～

After church I rush to the store. Tom said not to worry about bringing anything to the picnic, but I still think I should. Is it a sin to buy a pie and pass it off as your own? Probably. So I decide I'll buy a pie and leave it in the container from the store. I might be stingy with time and bad in the kitchen, people might think, but at least they won't think, *Hmm, this tastes like the apple pie from Save-Some.*

I drive to First Lutheran, which is on Second Street, and for some reason that cracks me up. I wonder if there is a Second Lutheran, and if so, is it on First? Who's on first? Could it be First Methodist, or maybe it's the Second Baptists? Really, now, who's on first?

I park and walk around back, following a family of five with one double stroller. The dad is pushing the stroller and the mom is holding

LARKSPUR

the hand of a boy who is probably five or six years old. He's jumping over every seam in the sidewalk and yanking on his mom's arm to try and get her to do the same, which she does. This cracks me up, for some reason, and I wonder if I'll be the kind of mom who does stuff like that.

Tom sees me first and comes over. "Hi, I'm glad you're here." He gives me a weird side-hug.

I side-hug him back as he takes my Save-Some apple pie.

"I said you didn't have to bring anything, but thanks," he says.

"Yeah, I debated passing it off as homemade and figured I shouldn't."

He laughs at me as we walk over to the dessert table. Then he turns us toward a plaid blanket under a tree, waving at people and smiling.

Tom leans over and says in a low voice, "Do you see the woman in red by the pecan tree?"

I recognize there is only one woman in red, not that I'd ever have guessed it was a pecan tree. "Uh, yeah," I say. She's at least eighty and wearing matching red pumps.

"She's Sylvia Sather. And she makes the most amazing desserts. Everyone always tries to get whatever she brings, because it's always good."

"Nah, she probably just gets her stuff at Save-Some," I tease.

"Really. And today, I got a piece of some sort of chocolate meringue pie she made. It's over here." Tom moves a little to the right and I see the stashed slice of pie, just visible next to the tree we're under. He's right, it does look good. I sit on the plaid blanket, glad that it's warm enough for church picnics.

"How'd you manage that?"

"Benefits of getting here early to set up tables." He grins.

The boy who was hopping over sidewalk cracks comes over and says, "Hi, Tom," and plops down right in my lap with a great deal of force for a child who can't weigh much.

"Hi," I say and introduce myself.

"Your name is *Lark*?" he asks, as if I said my name was Booger or something.

"Yeah. It gets worse. My real name is Larkspur, and it's a kind of flower."

"I'm very sorry to hear that. My name is Alex."

I compliment him on his nice, normal name and he stays in my lap. We eat fried chicken, and I try not to drop crumbs into his sandy hair. He gives me the occasional bite of potato salad, and I quickly discern it's not because he's into sharing. It's because Alex really dislikes the potato salad that one of his parents put on his plate.

"So, Lark, are you Tom's girlfriend?"

I smile at him, as he's turned around in my lap to see my reaction. I smile wider, put a bite of chicken in my mouth so I don't have to answer, but I also shake my head no.

Tom tells Alex this is our first date.

Alex doesn't miss a beat. "So, you gonna kiss her?"

"What do you think?" Tom deflects the question.

"No. I think Lark's nice and all, but girls are too gross to just go around kissing. I mean, your mouth *on* a girl's mouth. What a weird thing to do. There's this girl in my class—Savannah—and she tried to kiss me on the playground. She was really close when I ran away, but I think I could guess what that would be like. I mean, she didn't even *touch* me and it was gross, and that's why I ran really, really fast."

"Did she chase you?" Tom asks.

"Yeah, but I was too fast." Alex cranes his head to look at me for a second. "You're prettier than Savannah."

"Thanks, Alex," I say and plant a big, smacking kiss on top of his head.

"Huh! That wasn't gross." But he still flees, showing us how fast he can run, all the way back to his parents and their double stroller.

Tom waits until Alex is long gone to pull out his precious slice of chocolate meringue pie from behind the tree. With a great show of chivalry, he offers me the first bite, on a white plastic fork. And suddenly, eating off Tom's fork, I realize that this is one of those rare dates where something has "clicked" and it feels like I've known the person for much longer than I really have.

It is also the most amazing chocolate experience I've quite possibly ever had. The chocolate tastes like a thick pudding, but richer, and the light meringue is airy, and has those little mysterious drops of gold on it.

"What do you think those little gold drops are?"

"I don't know, but they're good."

"Little mysterious drops of gold can only be good, even on pie."

And Sylvia Sather's crust is better than the crust on Mrs. Smith's frozen pies, and that says a great deal. I adore Mrs. Smith, but she is now firmly in second behind Mrs. Sather—from First Lutheran on Second. I take advantage of Tom's talking to eat slightly more than my half of the slice. He's leaning on one elbow, sprawled on his red and blue plaid quilt, telling me about his career aspirations.

I tune out to silently hallelujah that this is my life. What a moment. What a man. A man who is feeding me chocolate pie with little golden dew drops is telling me that he is working on "making detective," however that happens.

"...I'm really glad I stopped you the other day," he's saying, and I snap back to attention.

"Me too," is all I can come up with. I'm moving past silent hallelujahs to full-blown silent prayers of thanksgiving, which are more distracting.

"Your mom is quite a lady. She was surrounded by all this stuff—feathers and glue guns, when I got to her house the other day."

I smile, because anyone who meets Mama realizes she is "quite a lady."

"No telling what that one's about. Last year she got into the business of embellishing flip-flops. She hot-glued everything from dice to feathers on them, tied bows and bells on them, and anything else she could think of."

"Did she sell them?"

"I think she meant to, but then she and her Sunday school class ended up wearing them and giving away the rest. If you see a woman in truly outlandish flip-flops, they're probably Mama's. She's always doing something wild."

"Like what she's doing for you?"

"Well, there's that."

"Why are you okay with your mom being so involved in your life?"

He doesn't beat around the bush much. "I'm not okay with my mom being so involved in my life. I'm okay with my mom being really involved in an area or two of my life. The rest is off limits, and she usually respects that. I wasn't getting anywhere finding dates on my own, and it's an area that's long been neglected."

I can't help but think that my love life was like Brant's primed, stark white walls—thirsting for life, color, change, attention, and not getting it. "So if Mama's there to help, I decided this could be one of her areas."

"And now?"

"Now what?"

"Now that you're here with me and you've been blessed with half a piece of amazing pie, is she still needing to find you dates?"

"Uh, well, that's a little soon to answer, don't you think?" *Ah, but look at those eyes on Mr. Almost Detective. How cute is he?*

"I don't think so. I don't mind telling you that I like you a lot."

"I don't mind hearing it," I simper. I *simper!* I must really be getting good at this dating thing.

Alex and his family walk by just then, and he tells me good-bye. He's a few yards away when I hear him tell his mom, "That's Lark. She's a good kisser."

I cringe and don't dare to turn to his mother to see if she's looking for an explanation. Tom laughs and waves good-bye in her direction.

We get up and shake the quilt out. Tom says he is free to leave since he is not on clean-up duty. He walks me to my car and surprises me with a kiss. It's not too long, but longer than first-date church-picnic expectations had allowed. And as far as kisses go, it is quite nice. "Alex was right."

I nod, dazed, smile a good-bye, and leave, careful not to speed in case he's watching.

9

At three o'clock, I find Brant standing in front of his orange popsicle-ish sunset and tilting his head to the right.

"What's wrong?" I ask, stepping into the room without knocking. I hand him the left side of my purple popsicle and tilt my head to the right at the same angle.

"It's not quite right. This side is smaller than the other side."

"Yeah, I wondered when you said you could freehand it, but I can't tell now. It looks even to me." And that was weird, for him to freehand it, when everything else takes so much thought and planning.

"How were all your dates?" he asks without taking his eyes off his flawed semicircle.

"Oh, they were great! The first guy gave me his job, one guy cancelled, and one guy gave me half a piece of the most amazing chocolate meringue pie that I'll probably ever taste."

My enthusiastic answer at least gets him to take his eyes off the wall for a moment.

"That's all you want? A guy to give you a job and a piece of pie?" He's teasing, I think, but I don't mind.

"Sure. What else is there?" And while he finishes my purple popsicle, I tell him about my new position as Coordinator for Classes.

"What do they do on *Trading Spaces* whenever they need a semicircle?" he asks.

"I don't know. I quit watching it when the hot carpenter left." *I have got to learn to keep my mouth shut!*

Brant laughs at me and tosses his purple-stained stick at me. "I have an idea."

I watch with great interest as he closes the blinds, the front door, turns off the lights, and drags over a table to set a lamp on. Then he takes the shade off the lamp, exposing the bulb. Flipping the lamp on, we stand there in the odd light, looking at each other.

He's thinking of what to do next, and I'm just looking at him. His eyebrows rise slightly, then he heads toward the kitchen, returning with an egg. He hands it to me to hold, fat side up, in front of the light. It casts a semicircle-ish shadow over our orange popsicle semicircle. It isn't a good match and, wordlessly, he hands me other circular things to hold while he inspects the curve of the shadow—sometimes adjusting the lamp or the angle before ruling out semicircle models. We silently reject the egg, a saucer, a plate, a circular throw pillow (which must be new), and eventually find our perfect match: a light bulb.

I hold the light bulb up carefully while Brant fills in with a paintbrush dipped in orange. The lines in his forehead bunch up with concentration, and I don't think he's noticed the lack of conversation. Once he's satisfied he turns and asks what I think.

"It's perfect. And we can talk now, right?"

"Of course." He gives me a funny look, as if the last 20 silent minutes in which we solved this problem entirely nonverbally were somehow only unusual to me. Right.

"Great." But I can't think of anything to say. I start taping off woodwork in the dining room and another 20 minutes slide by silently. I jump when Brant walks behind me with a dropcloth and rests his hand on my back, just below my neck.

"Uh, sorry. Um. Do you want to get dinner with me later?"

"Sure. But first you have to decide on a color for in here."

"I already have." He looks so proud, it's cute.

"And...?"

"Red. Not red like a popsicle, but red like the berries on the shrubs outside in December."

I'm impressed, I admit it. "And do we have that particular red?"

"We do now. I went and got it when you were...well before you got here."

"Is that when you also got that *circular* pillow?"

He nods.

"It's nice. What else did you get?"

"Check the kitchen. It's all in bags still, and if I didn't get it right, tell me and I'll return it."

"Do you *like* what you bought?" I ask as I head to the kitchen. When he nods, I wonder why that isn't enough.

Brant doesn't seem insecure, or as if he doesn't really know who he is or what he likes—but I can't figure out why someone who knows himself would fill a house with stuff he hates. It's been bothering me.

Through the beige plastic bags I can tell he's gone with an orange color scheme. And he was obviously on a roll.

"I love this!" I hold up a rug (oval shaped!) that is striped in wavy lines of yellow and crimson. It looks like a psychedelic Easter egg. Next are a few pillows. I'd never buy them, but they look like what I thought Brant's style could be, and that makes me hopeful he isn't suffering an identity crisis after all. One large circle mirror sits on the countertop beneath the bag. Its frame is crimson, and will look great on his yellow walls.

I turn to tell him he did a great job, but he's right behind me. I end up stepping on his foot, which makes us both laugh for some reason.

"Sorry! I—oh, look at *that!*"

Behind Brant, on the opposite countertop, is a huge vase. Well, I think it's a vase. I don't know what you'd call it because it's so round and large, it's more like the shape of a basketball. And it's orange, of course. Popsicle orange. It has yellow, red, and turquoise ovals on it, but they're pretty small.

"That wasn't there a second ago, was it? I mean, how did I miss that?"

"No, I just put it there. Testosterone level is fine, by the way," and he smiles with those ridiculously cute dimples.

"Thanks for the bulletin, but I wasn't wondering."

He had filled the small opening at the top of the basketball-vase with white and yellow daisies. I'm so impressed, because that particular vase would look just as great without flowers.

"It's all so *you!*"

"Not the daisies," he says quickly. "I got those because of you."

"Well, they're not picked from Mrs. Huttle's yard, and they're not *for* me, but they're *because* of me. That's kinda nice, too." I'm teasing him, but he's not smiling, I notice.

"Lark, I'd give you flowers if I thought you'd take them from me."

I have no idea what he means by this. I picture him handing me flowers and me crossing my arms and sternly saying, "No." As if I'd do that! And a nice thank-you it would be for all my work over here, too!

"Okay. You know I don't look like Danica, and I don't look like Blanca—"

"Who?"

"Nevermind, but I'm not so…so *un-girly* that I don't like flowers."

"Un-girly?" He's smiling again, but probably just because he doesn't understand what I'm saying.

I go back to taping off the baseboards in the dining room, and Brant arranges his accessories—his ode to orange—in the living room. I'm dying to look, because I know it's going to be great, but I don't. My femininity has been insulted and I should have seen it coming. It wasn't all that long ago he told me I reminded him of his sick cat. Remember that, Lark?

We don't finish painting the dining room until seven, but it's glorious. It is very December Berry, which was exactly what Brant wanted.

"Didn't you promise to feed me?"

"I wasn't promising to *feed you*. I asked you to have dinner with me."

"Same thing, and I'm starving." I go to his fridge, which has a bad smell, and then raid his freezer for popsicles. I eat a green one, sitting down on the plastic dropcloth in the dining room.

"You seem to be out of food," I tell him.

"I wanted to go somewhere with you—"

"No! I'm hungry and covered in paint, and my house is a long walk for a hungry girl. Can't you simply order a pizza?"

"You're kind of dramatic when you're hungry."

"Please?"

"Yeah. I'll even pick it up, so it'll be quicker. You can stay here if you want, since the driveway might be too much of a walk for you."

I snort, which he ignores, as he dials Pizza Hut. Actually, he doesn't dial, since it seems to be on speed-dial. Brant puts his hand over the phone and asks what I want.

"Anything."

He smiles at me, rolls his eyes, and orders one large pizza with all kinds of meat, and another all kinds of veggies. My favorite.

Brant washes paint rollers and brushes while I finish my green popsicle—which is great, but not very filling when you're hungry.

When I tell him the driveway is indeed too far for a hungry, overworked painter he leaves me on the dining room floor. It hasn't been long enough since he called and I'm sure the pizza isn't ready, but I don't say so. I'm hoping I'm wrong. And I wish I'd gone with him as soon as he leaves. If I had, I could snarf it down in the car on the way back.

I have the Beatles cranked up when he returns. I shout a prayer, thanking God for food, and amen-ing, as I run toward the still-steaming boxes. What a glorious fragrance!

"Want to eat outside?"

"Whatever."

Brant sets the boxes on the porch, pulls Cokes from under his arm, and puts them down as well. I'm halfway through my first veggie piece when I see what else he has. We're sitting side by side on his front step and on the other side of him is a vase of flowers. Really! *Flowers.* I stop mid-chew and wait. I don't care what reason he gives, but I should at least give him the chance to tell me.

"You're *very* girly."

Suddenly, I care what he says. And I'm *so* not girly, right now. I'm a big pizza pig, actually. But a tear slips down my right cheek anyway, and then I'm a teary, smeary moron. But I throw my arms around his neck anyway, and hug him, trying not to get my pizza too close to his right ear.

When I let go of him, he puts down his veggie slice and moves the vase in front of us. It's your standard clear glass kind, but it's filled with pink roses and tulips and even large pink daisies. White carnations and greenery break up all that pink, and it's so, so beautiful. He must have gone to get these before getting the pizza, and that seems so, so sweet.

"Thanks, Brant." I don't know what else to say, so I simply look at my flowers and eat, and ignore the second and third tears. Brant is nice enough to ignore them as well.

Like earlier, there's another silence. This one is my doing, and it's a comfortable sort of silence. I'm grateful he's the sort who can just go along with it.

We eat most of the large veggie pizza like this, silent, side by side, looking at pink flowers. Contentment is palpable. I want to sigh happy sighs, but I don't. I gather up the pizza boxes, kiss Brant's left temple, and go to the kitchen. *Thank You, God, for such a weird and unexpected friendship.*

"You kissed me." I jump, because the Beatles are still playing and I didn't hear him come in behind me. His tone is matter-of-fact, and I can't read his face at all.

"Uh, yeah, I did." I smile. "You gave me food and flowers and said I was girly. What did you expect?"

"If I'd expected that, I would have done it sooner."

I dry my hands on a towel and lay it over the edge of the sink I've been cleaning. It had paint in it that has finally succumbed to my scrubbing. "I don't know how it turned out that after all this time, we're friends. But I'm grateful for it. Weird at first, but it's turned out nice."

"So I'm your friend?"

"Sure. I don't have a lot of them, so you're pretty high-ranking, you know."

But he doesn't look like he knows at all. "So, tell your 'friend' all about your love life then."

"Okay, but only if we can go stare at pink flowers while we talk."

"You can stare at pink flowers while we talk; I'm eating a purple popsicle and looking at you."

I tell him about Tom, and the picnic, and Alex, which makes me laugh, so I have to tell him what he told his mom about me and kissing.

Brant laughs with me. He stops when I tell him that Tom kissed me, too, and agreed with Alex.

Seeing I might have taken our new friendship a little too far and confided way too much, I change the subject and ask Brant if he's been to the Art Center lately.

"You mean, you're going to keep seeing this guy, right?"

"Yeah, why not? He's really nice."

"No reason. No, haven't been to the Art Center lately." His face looks pinched, and I remember thinking the same thing about his mom. Yuck. I decide to try to repair it.

LARKSPUR

"I think I said too much, and I'm sorry. And—"

"No, you didn't say too much. Really." And his face returns to normal. "You can tell me all about Tom and whoever else you see. Maybe you'll need a guy's perspective sometime."

I'm so relieved. I just need to make a mental note that guy friends cannot hear about kissing other guys. They're too competitive for that, I guess. And I'll remember this because somewhere in the midst of orange and yellow and crimson paint fumes, Brant became important to me in a way I don't understand yet. I smile, but it's dark and I don't know if he can see me.

"Come on and I'll walk you home."

I'm surprised when he helps me up and doesn't let go of my hand, but it's so comfortable that I don't mind. *I love his...his thoughtfulness*, I think, as he cradles my flowers against his body with his free hand. There's something distinctly intimate in strolling from his house to mine through the dark, hand in hand with the scent of pink flowers all around us.

I walk a little slower, and so does Brant, as if this is a perfectly normal thing for us to do.

10

Today is the last day before I am officially a Coordinator. How professional does that sound? I'll have to dress like a grown-up, maybe even order business cards. But now, I'm still in bed in my Hello Kitty pjs, feet tenting the covers above me, creating a great niche for thoughts of the illusion of adulthood.

And thoughts of Brant: My Friend. I haven't seen a lot of him this week compared to our one weekend where we painted his living and dining room. He's been working late, and I've been dating the rest of Plains Point's men. But I have given him a lot of thought. And you know what? It would be so nice if he were a boyfriend. My whole arm gets the shivers when he walks me home and holds my hand. He called me "very girly" (my new, all-time favorite compliment), told his mother he liked me once, and occasionally flirts with me. *But.* There's the issue of his mother, whom he has apparently sworn to please with his choice of women—and that can never happen with me, our current status as "friends," and my rather hot dating life.

Namely, one Officer Tom Trace, whose persistence and charm have almost eclipsed Brant's. Tom, who isn't afraid to back up his flirting with declarations of serious like, and who also is perfectly capable of causing sensations of shivers with a mere touch or glance. Maybe I shouldn't be going by that, since I seem to be pretty easy to give the shivers to.

I kick back the sheets and jump out of bed, ready to take on my last day of blue-collar-dom at the campus bookstore.

I race through the day and even swing by Hazel's Hair Haven as a paying customer, this time. She remembers me, of course, and is glad I returned so she can even out my short patch.

"Your eyes sure are lit up today, young lady." She nods, glancing at my reflection.

LARKSPUR

"Are they? I start a new job tomorrow. Coordinator for Classes at the Art Center. I'm pretty excited, I guess."

"Oh, that's great. Well, you'll be busy. My granddaughter, Alison, takes classes in the summer there. That place is always hoppin'."

"Sounds like my kind of place." I smile, so glad John and I met and I now have the correct hair for the job. It's still short, but less severely so. Now it looks intentionally styled this way, and it's a great improvement.

Hazel tells me to watch out for little Alison, who will be in every watercolor class offered.

I'm having dinner with Tom tonight, before one last late shift at the Laun-dro-matio. Brant asked too, knowing I thought today was a day worth celebrating, but not until I'd already set up dinner with Tom. He settled for tomorrow night, and I'm glad I'll be able to tell him all about my first day.

Tom knocks on my door a little late, which I've noticed is normal for him. He kisses my cheek, and as we walk to his car I see Mrs. Huttle standing at the edge of her porch, looking pointedly at me.

"Why don't you go ahead, Tom? I'll be right there." I walk over to where she stands, hands on her hips, and watch as she waits for Tom to get further away.

"Larkspur, I don't like the po-lice poking around here." She says *police* with the emphasis on the *po*, rhyming with *mo*. I try not to smile, but she's just so cute.

"Yes ma'am. Did Tom, um, look in your window, or something like that?"

"No, but he walked by, and I don't like it."

I nod, trying to see her issue, but missing it. It's not like Mrs. Huttle does anything more criminal than watch too many game shows in there, anyway.

"From now on, I'd like him to honk when he pulls up out front. One honk won't disturb me too much."

"Certainly, Mrs. Huttle. I'll make sure he understands. Good night."

"Larkspur," she calls after me, and I turn back. "The flowers look very nice. Thank you." She nods, not looking at me, but at the flower beds I've filled with mums, delphiniums, coral bells, and stargazer lilies.

It's the first compliment she may have ever given anyone, and my "you're welcome" seems hardly adequate.

My affection for her is at an all-time high as I climb into the front seat of Tom's po-lice cruiser—I think I'll start saying it like Mrs. Huttle does.

"What did she say?" Tom asks.

"Oh, she said she wants you to stop going to the door for me. She'd prefer if you parked and honked once." It sounds cute now, somehow, but I feel the smile on my face falter under Tom's gaze.

It's his steely po-lice gaze, and I don't like being its recipient. Last week he fixed it on a waiter who made excuses when Tom said his steak wasn't cooked correctly, and that waiter had the same frozen look I probably do now.

"Why would she want me to show you such disrespect?" He doesn't even blink.

"Uh, I don't think it has anything to do with me. She merely wants her privacy, and anyone who visits me has to walk through her yard right by her windows. That's all."

Tom eases into the street, and I notice that he's going a little above the speed limit. Professional privilege, I suppose. At least he's dropped the subject, and the planes of his face don't look so hard anymore.

I didn't ask where we were going, and Tom hadn't told me, so I'm surprised when we end up at the good old Lake Eats. And even more surprised when Tom parks and as soon as my seatbelt is off, Brant opens my door. He even reaches in and helps me out by the hand—totally disloyal shivers. *Not that they mean anything,* I remind myself.

"Hi." I laugh at the surprise and thank him. He gives me a quick, small hug and I notice that he is parked next to us. Tom comes around to where we're standing as I ask if Brant's already had dinner.

"Yeah, I ate earlier. I just came to sit out there and watch the sunset." He points to the end of the pier I fell off.

Tom introduces himself, and they shake hands. Maybe it's only me, but they seem to be sizing each other up. And Tom's left arm possessively has my shoulder in a too-firm, not at all affectionate vice-like grip.

"Nice to meet you, Tom. You two have a nice dinner," Brant says and walks off toward the pier.

LARKSPUR

I shrug off Tom's arm and take his hand instead.

"He's a friend of yours?"

I nod, as casually and with as much disinterest as I can convey. The po-lice gaze is coming back, and I try to head it off.

"Did he know we were coming here?"

I have to say, at this point I wonder if Tom will ever make detective. "Tom, *I* didn't even know we were coming here, remember?" I ask, and he nods slowly.

"How long have you known each other?"

"Since birth. So, tell me about your day."

And he does, thankfully.

Unfortunately, we are seated at a table where Tom has a view of a cobalt blue swordfish mounted on the wall behind me, and I have a view of Brant watching the popsicle orange sunset at the end of our pier. Perfect Lady is coming back from an afternoon sail, and her skipper tosses Brant a rope as he docks.

Tom tells me about how many speeders he stopped, one domestic violence call, and a drunk driver. It doesn't sound like a job I'd ever want. I admire him for doing it and tell him so. Tom smiles, and his charm, which had been absent all evening, comes out in full force. Ha, ha, full force. I crack myself up.

Anyway, I like the way he's talking about fishing with his dad and wanting to be a detective like him as well. He asks about my first day of work tomorrow, and I tell him the little bit I know. It makes me nervous to realize how little I truly do know about the position. But, oh well, I'm in love with the title at least.

It's a nice dinner, except I keep wishing I were sitting somewhere else, silently enjoying a sunset, instead of being in the conversation I'm in. And I should have continued thinking and should *not* have started talking. When am I ever going to learn that?

"You know what, Tom? This isn't working."

He looks at my icky shrimp, and I see he doesn't understand. But I've already started. "I mean, you're great and all, but we're not that great together. Thank you for dinner." *Wow, that came out badly!*

"You're...you're breaking up with me?"

"Uh, well, you could say that, I guess." I didn't think there was enough to "break up," but at least he doesn't think I'm talking about the shrimp anymore. The waiter comes at that moment, God bless him.

"It's him, isn't it?" Tom says. And even though he points in the wrong direction (nope, never making detective), I know he means Brant.

The waiter pretends to dig in his little book for credit cards and not listen. I'm simply glad he's still standing there, not that Tom has noticed.

"No, no. I told you we're just friends. But I will catch a ride with him since he's here and all. Thanks, Tom." I pat his hand and get out of there, relieved, but feeling so dumb that I didn't think it through any better.

I run out to the end of the pier and plop down next to Brant, who is clearly surprised. The adrenaline of dumping Mr. Po-lice on a whim is still pumping and I'm out of breath. "I'm glad I didn't miss it."

Brant glances at me, then asks, "Miss what?"

"The end of the sunset."

"Oh." He nods, his feet swinging over the edge of the pier. He seems to be deep in thought. "Good timing."

We sit there, silently watching, side by side, and listening to the gentle lapping of the lake water below. At least 20 minutes pass before Brant stands, offers me his hand, and casually throws his arm around my shoulders as we walk back to his car. I'm glad to see the parking spot next to Brant's is empty. This shoulder-holding stuff isn't as great as hand-holding, but Brant's still pretty good at it.

"You know, the food at that place is really bad. If we come here again, let's just watch the sunset and eat somewhere else."

"What about the oysters?"

"Oh. I bet they'd be better at any other oyster serving place in town."

"We'll have to try out that theory."

"If you like oysters here, you'll probably adore them anywhere else. Oh! I didn't even ask if you'd take me home," I realize out loud.

He squeezes my shoulder and opens the door. "It's okay. I'll take you home, Lark."

11

Standing outside the Art Center is a truly eccentric flamingo. I wonder if one of the kids' classes made it, and I admire its custom paint job, glued on wing feathers, and argyle necktie hanging from its neck. There was one outside a business down the street, too, but I didn't get a good look at it.

Unlike the flamingo, I arrive at the Arts Center looking totally, well, coordinated. My navy skirt suit is flawlessly pressed, and a pink silk shell peeks from underneath my jacket. My navy slingbacks are scuff-free and my hair, thanks to Hazel, looks amazing. I am the epitome of Coordinator, I think. And I'm even early—how cool am I?

My "impress the boss" interview was a joke, and it amounted to little more than a handshake and a "see ya in a couple of weeks." The boss's name is Gina, and she assured me John is such a perfectionist that he wouldn't have suggested anyone she wouldn't hire anyway. And she told me that even though he didn't know she knew, she was well aware that he'd been looking for a replacement for awhile, so it wasn't like I was the first person he came across or anything. I liked her right away, for her laid-back attitude. When I left, she'd even said, "Welcome to the family." Who says that?

"Uh, Lark?" I turn, not having heard John come in behind me.

"Hi! Good to see you!" He's dressed very casually, in paint-spattered jeans and a kelly green T-shirt.

"You look, well, nice."

"Thanks." I can tell he isn't approving, but I can't tell why. "Am I in the right place?"

"Yeah, totally. This is it. But I guess I didn't tell you that a lot of the times you'll be pitching in to help the teachers. And the kids won't mind splashing paint on you." He points to his jeans. "I'm sorry, Lark. Why don't you go change and come back real quick? Do you live far?"

"No, no that's fine." I, the overdressed Coordinator, am dismissed for dress code violations one minute into my new job.

Fortunately, it isn't an indication of the rest of the day, and once I have adjusted my outlook and my outfit, I can't wait to get started. The rest of the day is fantastic. I am indeed spattered with paint by the time I leave, having loved every messy second of it.

I met all the teachers, helped Gina with a paper jam in her printer, learned how to schedule the next season's classes—I think—and helped one teacher named Brenda manage an unruly acrylics class.

At the end of my first day at the Art Center, I'm sitting at home with my feet on the breakfast bar, waiting for my toenails to dry. I tried Sea Shell Pink this time, and it's a huge improvement over Pink Electrocution.

I'm tired of the project with Mama. Maybe it's time to downsize it to one night a week. Or call it off. Life before wasn't so hot in this area, but now it's all so forced, so contrived. There are only so many times I can bore myself with going through the mundane get-to-know-you details with someone. My own details bore me, and all of theirs started to sound the same a long time ago.

Where is just one guy who will come in, be different, and sweep me off my feet? Can't it be like that, instead of a Man Marathon? "Huh, what about *that* way, God?" I ask aloud, halfheartedly waiting for any input from above.

Someone knocks loudly on the door, and I jump, knocking Sea Shell Pink to the floor. Well, serves me right for such irreverence. At least the lid was on tight. I open the door to see Brant—who looks great—and try to not let on that I'd forgotten about dinner with him.

"Here," he says and holds out a fuschia vase filled with fragrant white roses. There are more than a dozen of them, and some are only beginning to unfurl their pretty petals. They're beautiful, and as unexpected as he is.

"Thank you! Come in. Are these because you didn't want Mrs. Huttle to make you pick tulips again?"

LARKSPUR

"No," and he looks insulted. "Those are for your first day at the Art Center. But she did compliment them as I walked by her porch."

"She didn't mind you walking back this way?"

"No, why would she?"

"Never mind. Let's go. I was too nervous to eat lunch, and I'm starving!"

I set the roses in the middle of my kitchen counter and give them one last admiring glance before grabbing sandals and heading out the door.

We try a new seafood restaurant to test out the oysters-are-better-anywhere theory and sit outside under a blue-and-white-striped umbrella. The breeze toys with the umbrella, and fresh grass clippings swirl at our feet. Maybe it's that I'm hungry, but those grass clippings smell divine.

Brant asks me so many questions about my day and my new job—and seems very interested in my answers—when he changes the subject. At least, I think he changes the subject. Hard to say since I don't know what he means when he asks, "What are you looking for?"

I scan the courtyard where we sit. "More specific, please."

"Your mom is going to a lot of trouble and you're seeing a whole lot of guys. What is it you're looking for, and are you going to know when you find it?"

My thoughts exactly, Brant. He has blown my theory that men don't do "deep" and stay away from topics such as these. But then we're playing the "I'm-your-friend-and-you-can-talk-to-me-about-other-guys" game, too.

"Well, I wasn't looking for a job, and I got one that's great." I'm stalling here, since I don't know how I want this conversation to go. "Uh…what I *am* looking for…" I refuse to tell him I want to be swept off my feet. I will not let those words escape these lips! "I guess I'm looking for someone I really admire and like to spend time with, to talk to, to fall in love with."

"You mean none of the guys you've met are options? Statistically, I find that hard to believe."

And *there's* the man in you talking. *Statistically!* There's a word that should not have entered a conversation about love.

"A lot of them seemed the same to me. A few of them I didn't like…a lot of them, really. Some weren't as available as they first appeared. Some

84

were okay until the next date; then I realized I didn't like them. And one lasted a lot of dates before I realized I didn't like him enough. Or maybe it was that I didn't admire him. I don't know."

"Let me guess—the jealous police officer?"

"Not jealous, but yeah."

"Jealous, trust me."

"Why do you think that?"

"He gave me two speeding tickets today, Lark."

"What? You don't even drive fast!"

"I know. One was for one mile over the speed limit, and the other was for two miles over the limit." He gives his most charming, dimpled grin and adds, "My insurance rate is taking a beating for you."

I don't get why he's smiling as if this is funny. Tom must have been following Brant around all day to ticket him twice since last night.

"I'm sorry! Want me to talk to Tom? It sounds like harassment."

"No, it's fine. I'm driving a little slower, and I'll take care of it, should it come to that. You didn't say how you'd know when you found it."

"What's so hard about that?"

"What's so wrong with me?"

The breeze seems to stop blowing at that moment, and the air gets very still. My napkin slips from my lap, but I don't reach down to get it.

"Um...nothing." *Nothing at all! Been thinking that myself!*

"Then?"

"Then, fine. I've thought about you. About us. About how your mom dislikes me so much and you've sworn to only get serious about someone she'd approve of. And, really, Brant, I think that's weird. I've also thought that I'd hate to let you get very close just to have you end it when your mom finds out."

"Oh." I can tell he didn't think I'd be that direct. And half of it I hadn't worked out in my head first, but it made sense when I said it, and it's true. Mrs. Stephens is the only thing keeping me from wishing for an all-out Brant pursuit.

White roses in a fuchsia vase! Now there's a man who could sweep me off my feet, and with very little effort!

"And if my mother were not a factor?"

85

"Then what would you do?" I turn it back around on him.

"I'd ask you out every chance I got. I'd give you flowers and popsicles and think up dumb reasons, like house painting, to have you over all the time. I'd hold your hand and flirt with you and try to make you love me."

"Oh..." His words somehow make the air leave my lungs, and I only get it back with a concerted effort. Oh, and he does all these things, and I didn't *get* it? "So, your mom is not a factor?"

"Never was."

"What about the 'friends' thing?"

"It was sincere at first, then convenient when you were seeing the other guys. And you are my friend, but I've never been satisfied with that." He takes my left hand then and holds it, sending serious shivers up my arm. Not that they mean anything. But still, wow. I'm so swept. "Let me explain the thing with my mom. I can understand why it sounds so bad."

He's still holding my hand, and I try to concentrate on what he's saying instead of his hand. It's difficult.

"Five years ago my dad left her—very suddenly. He'd been seeing someone else for a long time, not that we knew it. Mom took it hard, as you can imagine. After running into him and his new girlfriend at the grocery store, she decided to move to Santa Fe. She didn't ever want to run into him again, so that was her answer."

"Pretty dramatic solution. Did she know anyone there?"

"No. She found a psychiatrist, antidepressants, and gradually she found a whole new life out there, but it was really a dark time for her."

It's so hard to picture her as vulnerable as what Brant's describing.

"I went out there almost every weekend to help settle her in and check on her. She needed me, and I was there as much as I could be. I did anything she asked, if I thought it would help. So when we were talking one night and she asked if I'd make sure I had her approval for anyone I dated seriously, it didn't seem like a big deal. I said yes to make her happy and had all but forgotten it until she mentioned it the other night at dinner."

"She clearly didn't forget."

"No, and I'd still rather win her over than tell her I'm going back on my word."

This worries me, since I'm fairly certain there is no "winning her over" when it comes to me. Then Brant will be gone. And I only just got him tonight!

"Lark, I still see her like she was a few years ago. She's not as tough as she likes people to think. She's vulnerable and easily upset, and I'm not eager to wreck her newly found peace if I can help it. I helped her work for it, and I'd like to see her keep it. It's a tough balance, but I think we can figure it out together."

"Really? Because I don't think she's going to go for me. And then what? You say, 'Okay Mom, forget her,' so you don't wreck her newly found peace?" I keep my voice quiet, since I know my words are going to have some bite.

"No. I want her happy, but not so much that she can run my life. I promise." He smiles, leans over, and kisses the tip of my nose. Serious chills. Disorienting, thought-scrambling chills, because I have no idea if what he said is really enough. After all, he wanted her so happy that he lived with lots of ugly furniture, even though she was in another state.

"Hang on a sec." I pull out my phone, and when Mama answers, I say, "Mama. It's time to stop with the Man Getting Project. Thanks! If you've set stuff up, can you cancel, please?"

Brant flashes me a smile and picks up my napkin for me.

"That's great, Lark, but who is it?" Mama asks.

"Oh, I'll tell you some other time, but we're having dinner now and agreed to start this thing off with minimal maternal involvement. Um, no offense, Mama."

"None taken, baby." And she means it, because she's really happy. I can hear her yell for Stanley before her end disconnects.

We skip dessert and walk to the park nearby, hand in hand.

"You know, Brant, you never told me what *you* were looking for."

"You."

"No, really. Why now, after all the years we've insulted each other?"

"I could ask you the same thing."

"I thought I knew who you were, and had no idea how wrong I was."

"Sort of the same thing. I've wanted someone who wasn't pretentious, and lately that's the sort I've attracted. I didn't know you were so down-

LARKSPUR

to-earth and fun. That's what I've wanted, but we've been so busy disliking each other that I didn't see that side of you until that first night at the lake. No one else could be such a good sport about getting pushed into a lake."

"No one else could Macarena so badly that I'd end up in the lake in the first place. Not that I hold that against you. That's a good thing."

And under a willow with dancing, graceful branches, Brant pulls me in for a truly unforgettable kiss. I mean, weak in the knees, silent hallelujahs sort of a kiss. At least I hope they were silent. The willow swirls around us, making the whole park spin. Really it was the kiss, and not the tree that did that, but either way, I'm dizzy. And I thank God for this!

"I've wanted to do that for a long time," he says, but I wonder.

"How long?"

"Off and on, but it started the day you wore a miniskirt and a man's tie around your waist."

I'm confused for a moment, but it sounds faintly familiar. "That was…that was eighth grade!"

"No, seventh."

"Do you remember Inside Out Day?" I can't help but laugh as I ask.

"Yeah, the day everyone found out about my devotion to Spiderman. Come on, you know it made you want to kiss me!" And he leads me by the hand out from under the willow, laughing at the memory of his fourth-grade underwear on display.

The Beatles serenade us as we drive, and when we're almost back at my house a police car eases in behind us. Brant pulls over to the side of the road, red and blue lights flashing behind us, their reflections bouncing off the rearview mirror and coloring everything in the car.

"If that's Tom, I'm really mad now." My words don't match my mood though, I notice. I'm too happy to be mad, even at Tom.

"If that's Tom, let me handle it." And the look Brant gives me as the officer approaches says he's serious.

"License and registration, please sir," the officer says, without bending down. I know his voice, and I clamp my mouth shut with effort.

Brant hands it to him, for the third time today, and says nothing.

"Do you know why I pulled you over tonight?"

"Because you've been following me and doing this all day, and why shouldn't you get in one more stop before I'm in for the night?"

Tom drops his pen, bends to pick it up, and looks directly at me. "I thought he didn't have anything to do with us, Lark."

"Last night he didn't. I broke it off with you not knowing Brant and I would be more than friends. Tonight I went out with a friend, and it turned into our first date…not that we planned it that way."

"Yeah, sure."

Tom looks hurt, but I press on. "*And* I want you to leave us alone, Tom."

"I'm just doing my job, but I'll let you go with a warning this time, Brant. You were going one mile below the posted minimum speed limit."

Brant takes the yellow warning slip he offers and waits until the window is rolled up before saying anything. "One mile below the minimum speed limit? He must have it bad for you, Lark."

"I'd be careful, Brant. It all started with him pulling me over and giving me a little warning slip, too!" I hold it up and give it a shake before he grabs it.

"So, uh, I thought you were going to talk to him." I don't know how else to say it, and that's just how it comes out.

"Not in front of you I'm not. No man would respond well to that."

"Oh." Yeah, that squares with my limited knowledge of male psychology.

"I'll talk to him tomorrow, and if that doesn't go well, I know someone in internal affairs. I don't want it to go that way, but it might have to."

"You can't do that! Haven't you ever seen the TV shows where someone crosses a police officer and they all stick together and then you'll have the whole force harassing you?!"

"Lark, don't worry about it. And quit watching those shows, will you?" He's shaking his head at my prediction, but I wonder how inaccurate every single police show ever made could be.

12

I meet Christine at the park, reluctant to see what a StrollerMama Workout Guinea Pig must do. It sounds awful. I'm hardly qualified, having neither a kid nor a stroller, but I guess that hasn't stopped Christine. She waves me over and leads me in stretching exercises. I think she's pretending that I am an entire class, because she's speaking really loudly, and I'm right next to her. And she keeps addressing me as, "Ladies." Christine's always been weird, but I hate it when she's really publicly weird, like this.

"Okay, ladies, a deep cleansing breath please…and another…and we're warmed up and ready to go. Let's remember our posture, please!" She looks pointedly at me. Apparently I'm slumping. I straighten up, and we start around the walking track. Which is awful, because Christine has a stroller, and I'm expected to *pretend* I have a stroller.

I keep my hands out in front, like Christine, and wonder if what I said about her manipulating God was really bad enough to merit this kind of friendship. I think not, but she's my oldest friend and that probably obligates me all on its own.

"Lunges, ladies, are next!" Christine yells back, even though it's still just me, and I'm right behind her. "We're going to do half a lap more, then half a lap of deep lunges. Get ready!"

A woman and her dog hurry past, to get away from us.

"Your hips are your headlights, ladies! Remember that when you're thinking of posture!"

Right. Hips are headlights. Got it. After our half lap of deep lunges, we stop to check pulses, then the fun continues. To be fair, if I were truly plural, and "ladies" would thereby be fitting, then Christine would be doing a pretty amazing job. Well, and if I had a stroller. She's actually very confident and explains her exercises well. Who knew? Christine,

StrollerMama Extraordinaire.

My opinion of her skyrockets when we're done, and she hands me a bottled water from the little basket underneath her stroller's seat.

"You're good," I say, drinking as we walk toward a wooden bench.

"You sound surprised," she says.

"Yeah, but I shouldn't have been."

"I decided you were right about what you said the other day."

"About manipulating God?"

"Yeah, that. It's true. Really, I have this secret crush that seems impossible, and I just want God to deliver That One to me—not wait and be all holy and all for *The* One."

Secret crush? Oh, I love those words. "Who is it? Do I know him?"

"I'm not telling."

"I'm your oldest friend, you just told me you have a secret crush, and now you're not telling? I don't think so. I did lunges and pushed an imaginary stroller around this park for you, Christine. You're telling."

She takes a drink and scans the park. I look too, in case I might recognize Secret Crush Man. I glance right to left and am checking behind us when Christine laughs and tells me to stop. Okay, maybe it was a little manic, but this is big news.

"He's not here." She sighs dramatically. "He's in Rocklin, California."

"Where?"

"I think it's near Sacramento."

"But you met him here?" This is not making sense, especially the part about me not knowing about it until now.

"No...I haven't really met him."

"An Internet thing? Is that what—" But I stop because she's shaking her head.

"It's Mike," she says, as if I should suddenly know who she means. And I try—really—but I don't know a Mike, and I certainly don't know any guys in California.

"Mike Shaeffer." She looks at me, again waiting for me to understand. And strangely, now the name does sound familiar, but I can't figure out why. We didn't go to school with a Mike Shaeffer. We don't know anyone at church...not at work...not at..."OH MY GOSH!" I scream—

LARKSPUR

far louder than Christine when she was calling me "Ladies," earlier.

Christine shhhs me, and I lower my voice. "Your Secret Crush is the guy on the *radio?* The Air1 morning show guy? *That* Mike Shaeffer?!"

Christine nods and puts the lid back on her water bottle. I have no idea what to say. This is too weird, even for Christine.

"He's cute—I looked online. And he sounds so wonderful. Normal, you know?"

I know what she means. I've heard him talk about his lacking love life, and his desire to stick to a diet and lose a few pounds. He does seem like a nice, normal guy. But a nice guy in California. A nice guy in California she's never met!

"Uh, so what are you going to do about it, since manipulating God didn't work?"

"I'm thinking of visiting."

"Noooo! Christine, noo! That's, that's," I stop myself from saying "crazy," even though it fits. "That's very *Sleepless in Seattle.*"

"I know! Exactly."

"And you're Meg Ryan, and he's your Tom Hanks? Really, Christine? Yathink?"

"You're not being a very good Rosie O'Donnell here. She told Meg Ryan that it wasn't crazy."

"Christine! I am *not* your Rosie O'Donnell! I don't think this sounds good. I will not support a cross-country trip to stalk a radio personality."

"It's only halfway across the country. And I think he'd like me." She sounds so crushed. Her bottom lip protrudes a little, and I hate that.

"Of course he'd like you. I didn't say that he wouldn't. He'd be crazy not to like you, if, well, if he'd ever met you."

"He meets all those gorgeous famous Christian singers—the pretty girl-band types."

"Yet he's still lamenting his singlehood on the air every morning."

"I know! You see why I think he might be looking for a regular girl like me?"

I let the "regular girl" thing go, since she's hurting—not because there's anything regular about Christine.

"But you said you just wanted That One, not The One. There's a serious flaw in your thinking."

"Not if they're the Same One."

"Riiight. So, short of stalking and all, what's next?"

"Air1 is having a concert he'll be at, and I thought maybe we'd go."

This sounds much better than a drop-in to the studio. I mean, thousands of people go see those concerts and we'd probably never even get a glimpse of the guy. "So where is it?"

"In Albuquerque. We could be gone only one night, and it's next weekend."

I'm remembering the radio commercials I've heard recently, and remember the one she's talking about. It still doesn't sound like a great idea. "So, what if I say no?"

"Then I'll go alone in my beat-up, old car and forget to take my cell phone, and you'll wonder if I broke down on the side of the road and died. Then when I get back—alive and not speaking to you—I'll go stalk him in Rocklin, wherever that is."

"Oh." I hate it when she gets like this. "Well, I'm glad to see you're past using manipulation to get what you want."

⁂

Brant and I have finished our run when Christine pulls up to the curb. I asked him to run with me so I could be assured of a lingering good-bye kiss before our road trip. Pretty smart thinking, even for me.

"Morning!" she calls to us, since we're across the street.

"Hi, are you ready?"

"Yeah. Um, well. Do you think we could take your car, Lark?"

"Not with the tires it has now." The heat on the summer roads would be bad for any tires, and mine surely wouldn't make it. "This is last minute, even for you. What happened?"

Brant and I walk over, and I can tell that Christine looks really guilty.

"Well, the air conditioning went out."

"When?" Not that it matters, but I'm realizing what Christine already knows—that this particular road trip at this time of year is about impossible without air conditioning. Or unadvisable, at least.

LARKSPUR

"Last week." She looks neither at Brant or me, but sort of in our general direction. "I thought about looking into a rental, but didn't know how much they were."

"Why don't I drive?" Brant asks.

I spin around to look at him, but it's too late. Christine is already agreeing. Here I thought we had the perfect way out of this road trip. And we did, until Brant has to show how truly chivalrous he is.

"What?" I ask, but I'm merely stalling. I had a girls' road trip in my head, and one boyfriend/chauffeur is hard to instantly add into the mix.

"Really. I was worried about you anyway, and this way I won't have to." Then he puts an arm around me and kisses my head. "I'll go pack a bag."

It was far from the lingering good-bye kiss that I'd been anticipating, but maybe there will be other chances.

"He's really great," Christine says, and we go get my things. I nod, not listening to her talk about meeting Mike Shaeffer, because I have a bad feeling in the pit of my stomach. My geography isn't very good, but it doesn't seem like Albuquerque and Santa Fe are nearly far enough apart. They're definitely in the same state, and if I'm remembering correctly, the cities are within easy driving distance.

I kick my prayers into overdrive, first asking God to be in control of the whole Christine/Mike thing, and then, more fervently and less correctly, begging Him to make sure the weekend doesn't include Mrs. Stephens.

Brant is being a good sport about the impromptu road trip—even saying he'll pay for gas. The good sport part had lasted almost an hour when I realize his patience is wearing thin already.

Christine had to go to the bathroom before we got out of Plains Point, then 20 minutes later I needed to go. Which wouldn't have been so bad, except I'm extremely picky about where I will go and where I absolutely wouldn't ever dream of going.

Then there's also the rule I have about buying something from a store or a restaurant that you're really just using for a rest stop. I mean, it's not right to run into the Dairy Queen and use the toilet and not buy something. You've used several gallons of their water, their facilities, and in return, the least you can do is buy a bottled water. Except I also think this courtesy should be extended to those places whose toilets do not meet my standards.

And Brant stopped at no fewer than three places that did not meet my standards before finding one that did. It's not a pretty thing about me, and certainly not convenient, but if we're going to be together for very long, he was going to find out anyway. So I ended up with three bottled waters and a pack of gum—the waters might cause a repeat of this toilet search, now that I think about it, especially since Christine and I are doing an informal taste test, since I got three different brands.

Ray Charles is crooning "Georgia On My Mind" and I'm in the backseat—Christine stole the front when I was in nasty restroom number three—watching Brant cringe in the rearview mirror as she sings along. Finally he turns it off, rather than endure her vocals any longer.

"So, is one of you going to tell me why we're going to Albuquerque, or not?"

Christine turns around and looks at me. "You didn't tell him?"

She looks grateful that I didn't immediately tell Brant how insane I think she is. Actually I don't deserve her gratitude; I just haven't had a chance. "No. But go ahead."

"We're going to meet the man I'm going to marry," Christine says.

I don't think I'm imagining it, but the car seems to be slowing down. "Oh. Well."

I laugh at him, and he accelerates again, deep in thought, judging by the wrinkles forming across his forehead.

"So, Christine, has he proposed?"

"Brant! I said we're going to *meet* the man I'm going to marry." She looks at him as if this has cleared it up, which it of course has not. "As in, 'meet' for the first time. He doesn't even know me, much less that I'm his future wife."

Brant's eyes widen, then blink rapidly. I try not to snort.

"I'm driving you two to…ambush some guy, aren't I?"

"Yeah," we say, in unison.

Brant sighs, turns Ray Charles back up, but doesn't seem to notice Christine's singing this time.

LARKSPUR

It should be a six-hour drive, according to MapQuest, but that's without factoring in more rest stops than most normal travelers have in a cross country trip. Brant tells me—with a rather stern look that I think is cute—not to buy any more bottled water. We're in a little town just across the New Mexico-Texas border, and I'm walking down the street in search of a suitable bathroom. Christine is sitting in the parking lot, painting her toenails, and Brant is leaning his head back, covering his face with his hands for some reason.

When I return, Brant and Christine are discussing how bad her nail polish smells, and she offers to put her feet out the open window while he drives. "No. Really, no."

But after only a couple of miles, he shoots her a look and hits the button that rolls down her window. Christine giggles, stretches her legs out the window, and admires her new pedicure.

"Guess what it's called!" she yells back at me.

"Road Trip Plum?"

"No! Think more romantic."

"Road Trip Kiss?" I ask, mainly because that's what is on my mind.

Brant decides to join in and guesses, "Ambush the Groom!" He laughs and Christine doesn't.

"At First Sight," she says with a measure of reverence.

"Should be called At First Smell," Brant says, waving at the last of the polish fumes.

The novelty of a road trip wore off hours ago, and we're still an hour from Albuquerque. I suspect Brant had no idea what he was getting himself into when he offered to drive. Christine and I switched places, and she's snoring in the backseat. I'm staring out the window at our desert surroundings.

Brant reaches over and takes my hand, without taking his eyes off the road. After a few minutes, he raises it to his lips, kisses it, and softly says, "I must be crazy. I'm really glad I'm here with you, Lark."

I decide to overlook the first part of that sentiment, since the next part was so lovely. We drive like this, in complete peace for five minutes before I can't stand it any longer.

"Brant, do you think you could find a restroom?"

13

We get checked into our rooms and barely have enough time to hit a drive-through on the way to the concert. What Brant thought would be a six-hour drive took us nine. Christine and I had no such delusions and are just glad to have made it in time.

I don't bother to change clothes, since I only have what I'm wearing tomorrow left. Christine puts on a white, floaty peasant skirt with a few sequins at the hemline and a purple T-shirt. In small letters on her left shoulder are the words, *I'm her*. The letters are in gold, look homemade, and match the sequins on her skirt.

"Thought a lot about what you wanted to wear to meet him, didn't you?" I ask.

"Yeah, I'm nervous. Do I look okay?"

I do not tell her that she resembles an Old Navy model, or a misplaced Minnesota Vikings fan. I do not say these things because I am learning to think before I speak, and because she really does look nervous. "You look beautiful. Um, you do realize you might not get close enough to meet him, or for him to get the not-so subliminal message on your shoulder, right?"

"Of course I'll get close enough, Lark. So will you. I have two backstage passes! As soon as the show is over, we're to go to Door 7!"

I must be hungry, because my stomach doesn't feel very good suddenly.

We eat hamburgers while we drive and arrive with time to spare. Brant is able to get a ticket from a scalper at the entrance, and since seating isn't assigned, we'll all have bad seats together.

"All the people who didn't take nine hours to drive a six-hour drive already took the good seats," Brant explains.

But I'm too excited, and nervous for Christine, to do anything but return his teasing smile. Christine is already searching for Door 7, so she can be there when the time comes.

※

There are three bands, and I've heard of only one of them, but it doesn't matter. For one thing, we can't see much, and for another, well that doesn't matter either. It's sort of like a concert, but more like a seriously loud praise and worship God time, with thousands of people raising their arms heavenward. For the next two hours I relax and enjoy the music, eager to let my nerves slip away from me.

When the lights come up, Christine is already tugging me by the hand to Door 7.

"We'll meet you back here!" I call over my shoulder to Brant.

When we reach the door, there are dozens of others waiting with the same passes Christine is clutching. There are a few couples, but mainly girls—cute girls from mid-teens to mid-twenties, who for some reason, all look alike to me.

The door opens, and a large man in a black T-shirt ushers us in after checking passes. We file down a hallway and into a big room where the various musicians are standing around talking and shaking hands.

Christine walks ahead of me, then turns abruptly and almost rams her nose into mine.

"There…he…is!" she whispers, half an inch from my face. Her brown eyes look enormous at this range.

"So go say hello," I say, backing up so she comes back into focus.

Christine turns, and I don't follow so closely this time in case she has something else to say to me. We try to approach casually, and most certainly we fail at that. A group of 10 or so young women are surrounding Mike, and a collective giggle makes me wish we weren't about to join this group. I hang back further and notice that they look alike for a reason—they're wearing similar versions of what Christine has on. I had no idea this was the uniform for the Mike Shaeffer fan club, but it obviously is.

"Hi, did you enjoy the concert?"

I doublecheck, but that was definitely him talking, and it was directed our way. Christine spins to face me again, without answering, and turns her back completely on him. I grab her shoulders and spin her back. Her hair whips my eyeballs, and I blink back tears.

"Uh, yes," she manages.

I poke her in the small of the back, forcing her to join the girl circle.

"I'm Mike," he says, with a smile.

"I'm Christine, and this is Lark. We're from Plains Point." I'm proud of her. She said that really well, and the girl on her left even gave her a dirty look.

"I thought you were 'Her,'" he says with a laugh, pointing at Christine's shoulder. He doesn't mean to be cruel, of course. How could he possibly know that those words were intended for him?

"Oh." Christine giggles nervously. "I am Her. For someone, you know."

"Right." He smiles again, but clearly he doesn't understand her answer, and I don't think anyone else does either. Except maybe the girl in the red peasant skirt to Christine's left. She's a sharp groupie, that one.

When a girl in a yellow sundress starts telling a joke, Christine grabs my hand and we slip away.

"What are you doing?" I ask. "If you don't get back over there, you'll regret it and I'll hear about it forever, Christine!"

"No, you won't." I barely hear her, but I catch the sheen of tears in her eyes as she heads back toward Door 7. I hate that feeling when you're almost crying and you need to get out of a room before the tears fall, so I rush ahead of her, clearing the way and pulling her behind me.

When we make it to the hall, she looks up at the light, blinks a few times, and takes a deep breath. "Okay. Thanks. I'm good now."

"Where to?"

"Back to meet Brant."

I look at her, trying to make sure she's ready to walk away.

"Really, Lark. But I don't want to talk about it yet."

"Okay."

We make our way back to our seats, where Brant is staring up at the ceiling. I don't know if he's praying or studying the architecture, but

LARKSPUR

either way he misses the look I shoot him that begs him not to ask how it went.

"Hey! How'd it go with Mr. Right?" he says when he spots us.

Christine shakes her head. "He didn't get the memo that he *was* Mr. Right."

"Huh." Brant studies us for a minute, then puts an arm around each of us as we walk. "What a dummy."

Christine laughs, and my heart swells at his clumsy but perfect response.

Christine heads into the hotel room, and Brant and I linger on the shared balcony. The kiss I've envisioned all day is out of place now, with Christine's heart broken inside. Instead we settle for a hug, and I tell him who Christine's "groom" really was.

"Are you kidding?"

"No. She thought she was the future Mrs. Mike Shaeffer. To be fair, so did a lot of other women."

"Huh. To hear him talk on the air, you'd think no one was ever interested. Who knew Christian deejays get all the babes?"

I smile at him, since he's kidding, but I'm thinking about Christine.

"Well, not *all* the babes, I mean."

"Right, Brant. And that's such an endearing term, I'm forgetting to be flattered." But I'm not, and he flashes one of those smiles that shows off his dimples. "Good night."

"Night."

༄

Christine is pulling the covers up to her chin when I come in.

"I'm a moron."

"No."

"I'm a groupie."

"No," I say, and she pulls the covers up higher. "You were a groupie for about two minutes. Doesn't count. You aren't a groupie until you've tried it for a full 10 minutes."

"Good. Because that was a humiliating two minutes."

I sit on the end of the bed, cross-legged, and wait for her to talk. It usually doesn't take long for Christine to open up.

"Did you see the other girls?"

I nod.

"We were all almost dressed alike! How embarrassing. Did you see the one in the red skirt?"

I nod.

"Did you see her shirt?"

I shake my head.

"It said, 'I like Mike!' "

"Did it really? I missed that."

"I have no idea what I was thinking."

"I'm pretty sure it was, *Maybe he's the one and he sounds great, and I'll take a chance and meet him.* What's so bad about that?"

"What's so bad is that I should have known that if I have to tell a guy—in writing on my shirt—that I'm special, well, maybe I'm not. Maybe I'm just like every other girl. I *hate* being like every other girl!"

"Yeah, you're probably not used to that."

"No kidding! But tonight there wasn't anything special about me. I was merely another floaty skirt with a homemade shirt."

I try not to smile at the unintended rhyme. "Of course you're special, Christine."

"But I should have known that when I meet the man for me, I won't have to spell it out in gold letters. He'll know."

"Yeah. You're right. He will." Then I immediately wonder if that's true. I mean, people don't always know right away. Couples who know each other forever one day realize that the one for them is someone they've known a long time. I can't help but think of Brant. I never would have known he could be who he is to me now.

And who is he anyway? A fantastic boyfriend, but really, so was Tom for awhile. Too early to get excited about anything there, I guess. And, for that matter, the handsome Separatist was pretty great for, like, a few days. Maybe I'm a really awful judge of men. I must be. I know I'd have run off with a hot Scientologist, just like Katie Holmes.

Maybe the right man could even come up to me with the words, "I'm him," and I still wouldn't get it. Except it *would* be him. Then what? His friends would shake their heads about how stupid I am, and say, "What a dummy."

Oh, God, don't let me be a dummy and miss any of your blessings, I pray silently, eyes shut and head bowed. I mean to go on, since this is important stuff, but Christine kicks me from under the covers as she rolls over.

"Lark?"

"Oww!"

"Sorry. But get in your own bed. I'm tired."

"Oh. Right."

14

The sun peeks through the heavy hotel curtains, and I'm anxious to beat Christine to the shower. Last thing I want is for Brant to see me, if I look as grungy as I feel. I collapsed into bed last night in the same clothes I'd worn all day—the same clothes I'd gone running in that morning, even. I slept surprisingly well, considering how grossed out by myself I was.

Christine grunts a good morning at me as I leave the bathroom, and she's going in. Brant is standing on the balcony with a cup of coffee.

His greeting is much cheerier than Christine's. He kisses my cheek and asks if I want to run. It's a tempting thought, to run with him in a new city, but I shake my head. "Wrong shoes." I don't add that I'm not about to be as grungy today as I was yesterday, but that's totally the reason. Instead I stand next to him, shoulder-to-shoulder at the railing, and we watch the few cars coming and leaving the parking lot. Sometime in the night a light rain fell. Puddles dot the asphalt, and gray clouds loom.

"Have you thought about where you want to have breakfast? Christine should be out in a minute."

"We've been invited to join my mother, if you're okay with it," he says, looking at me to gauge my reaction.

I'm so good that I don't blink, or vomit, or anything. I just smile and say, "What a nice surprise. I didn't know she was in the area."

"She's spending the day shopping in Albuquerque and was surprised to hear I was in town. Don't worry, though—we won't stay long, since I know how long the drive is now." He bumps my shoulder softly to let me know he's kidding. As if I could have missed the dimples.

I try to smile back, and I think I succeed. Mrs. Stephens at any time of day is awful, but first thing in the morning on an empty stomach? *That's just not right. I mean, ick.* I hope Christine behaves herself. Or maybe not,

LARKSPUR

now I think about it. That could be totally amusing and make breakfast with the bunned, pant-suited Mrs. Stephens completely worthwhile.

"Hi, guys!" Christine emerges without a trace of sadness over the lost love of Mike Shaeffer. I have to laugh—only Christine could be lovesick and stage a multi-state trip to meet a guy, then the next day be fine when it didn't go as expected. She bounces back, that one.

Thirty minutes later, we're checked out of the hotel and pulling into the restaurant's parking lot. I'm shocked to realize the woman coming toward us is Mrs. Stephens. Her blond hair is loose and shoulder-length. In place of her usual silk, she's wearing jeans and, oh my gosh, Birkenstocks.

She looks like a normal person. Well, a normal person in Birkenstocks, which I personally detest, but not as much as buns and raw silk, lately.

I shut my mouth with effort as Brant kisses her and introduces Christine.

"And hello, Larkspuuur. You seem surprised."

"Oh? I do?" I so wish she hadn't noticed—that I'd been able to keep my mouth from hanging open.

"You must have been expecting a shih-nyon."

"A *what*?" I wish I knew what a *shi-nyon* was, because now she's looking at me as if I'm terribly uneducated.

"My hair, Larkspuuur."

Does she have to keep saying my name like that?

"A chignon. I usually wear it in a chignon."

"Oh, right. I just thought it was a bun."

"Never a bun, darling."

Well, at least she didn't call me Larkspuuur again. And the jeans and ugly hippie shoes, do those have fancy, pretentious names that we could whip out and make me feel stupid? Please, do they?

Mrs. Stephens asks what brings the three of us to her state—yeah, like all of New Mexico is her exclusive domain or something. I decide to stay silent and let Brant or Christine answer, since she asked all of us.

Christine shocks me by eagerly pouring out the whole story. She starts by asking if Mrs. Stephens listens to Air1, which of course she does not.

"No, Christine. I don't care for religious music." Which totally proves she is being truthful and has never listened to the station. Not that it was in question, of course.

"Well, I was sure one of the deejays on that station was my soulmate." Christine takes a sip of orange juice, then leans across the table toward Mrs. Stephens. "I've developed this huge crush the last few months, and we came out here to meet him."

"And did you?"

"Yeah. And he was just as nice and great as I thought he would be."

"But what happened?" Mrs. Stephens is riveted, and the two of them are talking like old friends. I hate it.

"I went up to him, said hello, and realized he's standing in the center of a whole group of girls just like me, with the same clothes, the same crush, the same everything. There wasn't anything about me that would make me any different. I was simply the next one in a parade of women."

"A parade of women. Hmmm."

"So we left. And I cried, but I decided that whenever I do meet my soulmate, I'll stand out from any crowd. Just because."

"Interesting, Christine." Mrs. Stephens butters her toast. "And you, Brant, offered to come along?"

"Christine's a/c went out, so that's how I ended up along for the ride."

Mrs. Stephens pats her son's hand. "Always chivalrous, you are. You have always had a soft spot for helping women in need."

Women in need? That's what we are? Oh, please.

"Excuse me, please." The ladies' room is calling this woman in need.

When I return, after deep cleansing breaths and a whispered pep talk to the mirror, telling myself to behave, I think I might need to return to the mirror after hearing Christine and Mrs. Stephens talking about a jewelry store in Santa Fe that they both love. But I do not return to the mirror, nor do I roll my eyes. I think. I discreetly deep-breathe and sit.

"Larkspuuur, you should really go sometime. I notice your accessorizing could use a lift."

"Ah, yeah. A lift." I might kill her. I might.

"The right jewelry can be especially flattering for plainer features."

"For…plainer…features?" I could not have heard that correctly. No one is that mean. She just called me ugly in front of her son? Her son,

LARKSPUR

who was busy paying the bill and apparently didn't even hear that? And Christine is busy trying to flirt with a guy in a Corona beer T-shirt at the next table. Mrs. Stephens' timing is impeccable, I'll give her that.

"Well, yes, Larkspuuur. You know, should someone have a particularly *common* appearance, the right accessories can do a lot." She smiles sweetly at me over her coffee mug, and I want to kick her shins under the table. Or stomp her Birkenstocked feet. Or—

"Lark, you ready?" Brant offers me—his plain girlfriend—a hand, which I accept with a glance at his mother. He pushes in my chair, and I hang onto his hand all the way out to the parking lot. Partly to bug his mother, and partly so I don't give in to my evil fantasies and start swinging at her.

∽

We're nearing Texas when Christine makes a gruesome discovery. Not like a body-on-the-side-of-the-road gruesome, but gruesome just the same.

We've switched places, with me in the back and her in the front, and she has amused herself by digging through the glove compartment and center console. In the glove compartment she laughed and made fun of Brant incessantly for actually having a pair of leather gloves there. And really, who has gloves in their glove compartment? The center console has the truly odd discovery, though.

"Brant! Are these yours?" Christine asks, pulling out a stack of CDs.

We've been listening to CDs he has in one of those sun-visor organizers, but these are of a distinctly different category. No Beatles in that stack. Brant tries to grab at them, but Christine switches them to her other hand and reads off the artists.

"Oh my gosh. Willie Nelson, Mary Chapin Carpenter, Lyle Lovett, Confederate Railroad...*Confederate Railroad,* Brant?"

"Hand it over, and I'll show you why I own that one."

Christine does, and a few seconds later Brant is singing the most horrible, hilarious country lyrics I've ever heard. The best part is the twang he adopts, as he belts out some crazy lyrics from the band's song, "Trashy Women." Brant flashes me a smile and sings about a high school senior who asks a cocktail waitress/Dolly Parton lookalike to the senior prom.

We crack up, and make him sing it two more times. Then he moves on to Lyle Lovett. Which is far more tasteful, as far as country music goes, but not quite as entertaining as "Trashy Women." Fascinatingly, Brant easily adjusts his twang to the more refined version that Lyle possesses.

And there, in the backseat of Brant's Mercedes, I fall completely in love with a man I've never met before. I must be as bad as Christine.

But when Willie Nelson and Julio Iglesias sing, "To All the Girls I've Loved Before," I'm a goner for Willie. Sure, it's a corny song, but sigh after contented sigh escape me as Willie's straightforward vocals contrast the more exotic Julio's. I'm moved by the sad story told by "Pancho and Lefty," but when he sings "Always on My Mind," the deal is sealed. I'm glad I'm in the backseat, alone with my minutes-old crush on a fantastic, aging, country music legend.

"So, Brant, why the secret stash?" Christine asks what I've been wondering.

"Did you see how you two reacted?"

"Yeah, but you're very publicly a Beatles fan and very, very privately a Confederate Railroad sort of guy."

"I probably don't have half as many surprising sides to me as you do, Lark."

I smile, remembering how I used to think he was boring and couldn't possibly be interesting or surprising in any way. I'm amazed at how wrong I was about him. I drop the subject, though, because I think he meant that as a compliment, and that's enough to make me shut up and smile. And then I really smile when he puts in someone named Mary Chapin Carpenter, who sings a saucy song called, "Shut Up and Kiss Me." As if that's not enough, I get a wink in the rearview mirror.

This moment—the one with the wink—was worth breakfast with Mrs. Stephens, and even worth her stupid insults. And how startling to realize that this man could be worth enduring that particular woman. This is my thought as I drift off to sleep, smiling, lulled by the guitars in music I've never before heard.

15

It's been two months since the willow tree swirled around us as Brant kissed me. As in, exactly two blissful months, and I want to do something special to acknowledge the successful end of Mama's Man Marathon. I refuse to consciously think in terms of "love," yet the concept seeps into my thoughts without permission just the same.

Brant and I have hardly mentioned his mother, and the threat I thought she would be hasn't materialized after all. Well, except for that one breakfast, but I can't count that. I mean, we were in her territory, and that won't happen again anytime soon. That's especially good, since after all that Brant said about her divorce, it's been harder to dislike her. And the way he was there for her, even though she moved away—those are nurturing qualities that are certainly attractive in a man.

Yet there's something I haven't wanted to dwell on. That she somehow got him to be so present, so attentive, and so agreeable—how can she really be "not a factor" any longer? That doesn't quite add up, so I don't think about it often. I'm just glad there hasn't been reason to.

I've kept Mama in the dark, too, just for good measure. I don't think she likes Brant, and it's probably too soon to tell her who I'm seeing. I didn't even tell her I was going away that weekend, much less with whom.

Brenda, my favorite art teacher, comes by my desk as I leave Brant a message.

She waits until I hang up before teasing me, "Okay, Lark-in-love, I know you're busy and all, but if you could lend a hand I'd be grateful."

"What do you need?"

"I have a stained-glass class with 10 12-year-olds, and I don't want any of them going home with Band-aids today. That's my goal, but I need more adult supervision to make it happen."

"You got it." I like Brenda, and I really like her stained-glass class, so I don't mind at all. We get through the two-hour class cut-free, and I help her clean up.

"So, what are you and the boyfriend doing?"

"I want to do something special, but I don't know what."

"The first thing I ever did for Carl was cook for him—as a surprise at his house." Brenda and Carl have been married for a year, and happily it seems, so I listen. Happily married for a year is heady stuff, you know.

"How did that work—did you break in, or what?"

"No, I cleared it with his roommate."

"I like the cooking idea, but not the 'at his house as a surprise' part."

"Just a thought," she says, "and if your plans fall through, call me. Carl's out of town with the youth group, and I want to see a movie, but I hate going alone."

"I'll remember that."

Brenda dumps a dustpan full of glass shards into a trash can, and I go to check voicemail, in case Brant has called.

He has, and I decide to run my idea past him. Well, Brenda's idea.

"I just have a second, Lark. What are you doing tonight?"

"I'll make it quick. How do you feel about a surprise of some sort at your house?"

"A surprise of any sort at my house would be great." His voice is growly and completely inappropriate. I love it.

"Stop that! Then it would be okay if you came home to me in your kitchen."

"If that's the room of choice, okay then." Good thing I've figured out he's kidding. "Key's under the mat. I'll be a little later than usual."

"Okay."

"And Lark?"

"Hmm?"

"I'm looking forward to seeing you."

"Me too. Bye."

I struggle to Brant's kitchen under my load of groceries, barely making it to the counter before the brown paper bag rips. I leave the spilled contents, crank up the stereo, and put on Brant's Kiss the Cook apron that I've never seen him wear.

LARKSPUR

Inspired, I printed the recipes at work for oysters, salmon in lemon cream sauce, and rice pilaf. I picked up all the ingredients, a chocolate cake, a box of popsicles, and if I hurry I can have it done quickly, since the oysters are raw and the salmon should be quick.

I'm half singing, half yelling Brant's favorite, "And I Love Her," and arranging my oysters on a tray when I hear a voice in the living room. I freeze. It's a voice that is definitely not Brant's.

"We just came in, darling—" Mrs. Stephens stops midsentence, and her mouth forms a straight line when she sees me.

"Hi," I say.

"Larkspuuur, what are you doing?" She raises her eyebrows and takes in the apron and current disastrous state her son's kitchen is in.

"I'm cooking, Mrs. Stephens." It's idiotic, but it's all I can muster. I've just noticed that the tallest, blondest, most beautiful woman I have ever seen is just steps behind Mrs. Stephens. "Hi, I'm Lark."

"Oh, hello, Lark. My name is Monique."

Of course it is. And with a French accent. Instantly my features feel "plain." As if Mrs. Stephens weren't bad enough all on her own!

"Where is my son?" There is a hint of accusation in the question, as if I have maliciously stuffed him into the walk-in pantry.

"He's working late, but should be home soon. Um, was he expecting you by any chance?"

"No, dear. I'm his mother, and that means he welcomes my comings and goings as they are. I don't get to come to town all that often."

Really? Oh my gosh, it seems like all the time. "Can I get you two something to drink?"

"No, I think Monique and I would rather look around at how much Brant's house has changed since my last visit. Truly, he must have had a horrible time lately, and this is how he's expressed it." Her words hit me square in the stomach, as she intended, I suspect, and she turns away with a look of disdain as she leaves the kitchen. Mrs. Stephens does disdain *very* well.

My shoulders come down a notch, with effort, after I realize they were scrunched up near my ears from tension. I silently repeat to myself, *Mrs. Stephens is not a factor. Brant said so.*

But I only half believe it, and even if that's true, what about the babe? Is she a factor? And how could she *not* be? My pep talk does nothing for me, so I start to pray as I fiddle with the lemon cream sauce. Maybe I should have started with that, because I'm so rattled I can't focus anyway. I clean the kitchen and strain to hear every word being said in the other room, but I only hear Monique's delicate trill of a laugh.

The lemon cream sauce burns. Which wouldn't be so bad, except that it burns so badly it stinks up the house. One stench summons another, in the form of Mrs. Stephens, who arrives to dramatically fan at the air with a cookie sheet. Which is *so* not necessary, but it successfully humiliates me, which apparently *is* necessary.

"Larkspuuur, dear, I don't know why you're here starting fires, but maybe you should leave now."

"I didn't start a fire, Mrs. Stephens. The sauce burned, that's all." I carefully arrange capers and dill over the salmon, since it won't be wearing lemon cream. Tears sting my eyes, and I focus on the fish so they won't fall.

"You need to leave. Monique and I are only here for tonight, and Brant will be so interested in seeing her that it wouldn't be much fun for you to sit and watch anyway."

I think of the night I had planned, and then see the night ahead. Me watching Brant drool over Monique—or try not to, good luck with that. Mrs. Stephens insulting my cooking and fanning at imaginary smoke. What's a two-month anniversary of a kiss, anyway?

"You're right, Mrs. Stephens." I smile sweetly as I take off Brant's apron. "I can see Brant any night, after all." Okay, that part was a little nasty of me, but I was due.

I say good-bye to Monique on my way out, and dial Brenda. Maybe a movie is a good idea after all.

Twenty minutes later I'm telling Brenda what happened, as she drives us to the movie theater, top down in a blue convertible.

"You were cooking what?"

"Oysters, rice, and salmon in a sauce that burned."

"Whoa. This is serious."

"Brenda! It was your idea—you said you cooked for Carl, remember?"

LARKSPUR

"I bought a frozen pizza that cooks at the same oven temp as the frozen fries I bought. Oh, and I got a new bottle of ketchup. That's as much thought as I gave it."

"Oh. Well, that wouldn't have impressed his mother, either."

"Sounds like nothing will, short of mile-long legs and a French accent."

"No kidding. You know, I want to cook amazing things. I want to be a better me and learn to like those little ball things you put on fish—capers, and…am I making any kind of sense?" I'm yelling since the top is down and Brenda's driving fast, but she's shooting me a confused look.

"No."

"Brant…inspires me. I want to be the best me that God made me to be, just for him. Well, mostly for him. But for me, too."

"Even if your best will never be enough for his mother?" Brenda's words cut.

"He says she doesn't matter," I say, pulling out that threadbare line I've been trying to get myself to believe.

Brenda nods, turns left, and eases into the parking lot. "If you believe him, why are you here?"

"Because she asked me to leave, and a night there sounded awful."

"But you were there with his blessing, and mom and Monique were not."

"But she's his *mom*. And she's…*Monique*," I say with an eye roll and an exaggerated accent.

"You sure you want to stay with me, or do you want me to take you back to your date?"

"There's no date, not anymore."

"Sometimes you have to fight for what you want, Lark."

"I *did*, and Mrs. Stephens spit me out with one look and a tall blond."

∽

The next day I skip my run and leave for work, amazed that Brant has not called. He hasn't emailed either, and I stomp out the door, sure that I am forgotten in the aftermath of Monique.

Mrs. Huttle stops me as I head toward my car. "Larkspur."

She has her hands on her hips, and purple old lady veins wind their way up her skinny arms.

"Yes, ma'am?"

"Those are new this year, am I right?" She's frowning in the direction of the tropical looking red cannas.

"Yes, they are." I don't add that they were on sale and I loved their flashy rainforest-looking foliage. They're pretty daring for West Texas, and I suspect too daring for Mrs. Huttle.

"They're harlots. Nothing but common garden *harlots*. Would you please dig them up when you have a chance?" She's shaking her head at the indecency of those red blooms and their broad striped leaves, and I try not to smile.

"Yes, ma'am. I'll be glad to do that after work." It's true they don't fit in with the rest of the cottage type flowers, but they're hardly "harlots"! Oh, I love that woman.

∽

I set my purse on my desk with a too-loud thump, which causes Brenda to stop in her tracks.

"What happened when you talked to him?"

"I didn't."

"You did the 'too busy to answer the phone' game?" She looks surprised.

"No, I didn't get to consider that game, since the phone did not ring."

"Ouch. Have you checked your email?"

My look tells her that I have, and she rushes back down the hall to shepherd her incoming students for the Mosaic Masters class.

I dive into the task of scheduling next quarter's classes, not that it needs to be done yet. But it beats re-checking my cell phone's ring volume and checking email every few minutes.

I should have known, really. Who tells his mother that her wishes in a suitable girlfriend are important anyway?

I knew that if I let Brant get too close, something like this would happen. It'd be great if he were more like me. I know the importance of keeping a mother at arms' length. Mama doesn't even know who I've been dating, and it works just fine for us. If Mama knew and didn't approve, it wouldn't be the end of our fledgling relationship. But Mrs. Stephens knowing and not approving certainly seems to be the end of us. What else could my phone's silence mean?

But then it rings.

I try to hide my disappointment when it's Christine's voice on the other end.

"Lark, I have a question."

"Uh huh."

"I've gone out with the same guy three nights in the last week, and I just want to know if that means anything to guys, or if that is only significant to those of us with ovaries."

I have no idea why this is the first I've heard of this guy. "Uh, I think that probably means something to them, too, but I can't say for sure."

"Oh." She sounds disappointed.

"So, who is it?" I'm interested, but I'm also trying to distract myself from thinking of the unanswered questions in my own love life.

"Hi name is Chad, and I met him at the bank." Christine's voice is as dreamy as it sounded when she talked about her Mike Shaeffer crush.

"How'd you meet? Does he work there?"

"No. He was in line in front of me. He wore one of those belts that said his name on the back and on the front he had a big, shiny silver buckle. I had to ask him what his name was since the beltloop in the back was covering up the "h." It looked like—"

"Cad," I fill in.

"Yeah. But it's really Chad. He's a farmer."

"Cotton?"

"Yeah. Um, Lark, would you mind if I don't introduce you for a long time? I mean, assuming this lasts a long time?"

"And why?"

"I don't think you'd like him, so why bother?"

"Why won't I like him?" What's not to like about a guy with "Cad" on his backside, anyway? I close my eyes in anticipation of whatever answer she's going to give. With Christine it could be anything. Um, he's a recent parolee. Or he plays imaginary musical instruments, or…

"Because you're so shallow."

"Because—*what?*"

"Yeah, you know how weird you are about looks. And Chad is wonderful, but he's not your typical pretty boy."

I start tapping a ballpoint pen on my desk, a tiny expression of my extreme annoyance. Not only is my boyfriend not talking to me after an evening with Monique, but now my best friend calls and tells me I can't meet her boyfriend because I'm too *shallow*? What is with that happening all in one rotten morning?

"Lark, are you there?"

"Yeah." It comes out sort of sharp sounding. Go figure.

"Well, um. Okay, I'll talk to you later."

I hang up without saying anything else, since I would rather hang up on Christine than open my mouth and let words come out of it at this particular moment. This is totally the right choice since some of those words running around in my head are so ugly they should never come out of anyone's mouth, much less mine.

Pretty boy types? That's so not fair. I try to remember the last time I dated someone who didn't fit that description. Then I try some more, and 15 minutes later I'm still trying when the phone rings.

It's him. I don't even consider the "too busy to answer" game. Well, and I'm at work, and I couldn't get away with that anyway. "Hello?"

"Hey, Lark. What happened to you last night?"

Hmm. Tell him his mother asked me to leave, or take the high road? "Went to a movie instead. Your mom said she and Monique were there for just one night, and you'd be busy with them. I figured she was right." I keep it light, but I wonder what his reaction will be to my mention of Monique.

"Yeah, we were busy, but I missed you."

"Busy?" Childish panic at possible interpretations of that one word.

"Well, we ate this fantastic dinner, and it was even later than I thought, but it warmed up just fine."

"It…it *warmed up* just fine?" The only thing nastier than raw oysters is

LARKSPUR

warmed up raw oysters.

"Sure. You know, Italian takeout from Ziti's."

"What about the oysters, and the rice, and the salmon?"

"Uh, I don't know what you mean. Oh, someone's at my door. I'll talk to you later, Lark."

At the click, I slam shut my cell phone. It doesn't satisfy, but there are children in the building, and my true reaction would endanger them, or at the very least, scare the pants off them.

Mrs. Stephens, who is *so* a "factor," trashed my seafood feast and served her son nuked Italian takeout. With a generous helping of French bombshell.

That really, really *bites*.

Brenda and Matt, a watercolor instructor, pass by later, and Brenda asks if I want to join her for dinner after work.

"No thanks."

"Got plans?" she asks hopefully.

"Nothing romantic. Just relocating harlots."

Brenda raises her eyebrows at this.

"Flowers. Just flowers, Brenda," I say, waving them off.

"Right. Call me if you need back-up on that."

16

I survey the red cannas, fists on my hips, feet wide apart. My mood is foul, and I'm tempted to just dig them up and throw them into the compost pile behind my apartment and leave them there to decompose.

I don't know what I was thinking. When the rest of the flowers' pale hues and delicate features blend for an English cottage look, why did I throw in a dozen crimson tropicals, all of three feet high? I narrow my eyes at the offenders—they look as out of place in Mrs. Huttle's yard as Monique looked in Brant's home last night. Just as flashy and foreign.

The knees of my jeans are muddied, and my face sweaty by the time I unearth the last one.

"Those are pretty." It's Brant, and I am not ready to see him. And so not ready for him to be complimenting the stupid red cannas.

"Inappropriate and all wrong in every way. Mrs. Huttle asked me to get rid of them."

"Where are you going to put them?"

"I thought the compost pile."

"You were going to throw them out? If that's the case, can I have them? They're really cool looking."

"Really? You want these"—I hold up a clump—"at your place? Are you sure about that?"

"Yeah, why not?"

"No reason." But it really stinks that Brant has appeared and expressed approval and *desire* for the harlot-y flowers I've compared to Monique. Maybe it isn't rational, but it bugs me, and I gather them all up and stomp across the street toward his house. "Where do you want them, Brant? Out front? In the back where no one will know you secretly want them?"

LARKSPUR

"What's with you, Lark?"

How do I explain? My shoulders ache with tension, my jaw hurts from all the clenching it's been doing, and I decide not to say anything.

Instead I start digging holes near Brant's mailbox. "What's with me?" I jam a canna into a hole and grab another one. "I made a seafood feast for you last night. Oysters, salmon, rice. I bought lip gloss and candles, spent ten minutes figuring out how to make your stereo stay on 'And I Love Her' so your favorite song would be playing when you walked in the door. It was a two-month anniversary of a kiss, and that was important to me for some reason." I force another canna into a hole and break its stalk, and the red bloom bends sharply, sickly toward the ground.

"So…what happened?" Brant asks, eyeing the cannas with what looks like pity.

"Your mother, who you say 'isn't a factor when it comes to us'—she happened! She shows up with Miss Magnifique, and then asks me to leave. So I do, and they trash my oysters and you didn't even know." I cram dirt around the base of a canna and fight back tears.

I only wanted to show Brant how great these past two months have been for me. I wanted him to feel special, and appreciated, and he was probably well appreciated—by Monique. The thought makes me sick. One thing is certain: I shouldn't have gotten so carried away, thinking it was so significant and all. What was I thinking? This hurts too much for that to have been a smart thing to do.

He stands there, not knowing what to say, it seems.

"Your mom is a big factor! There could be a reality show about her, that's how big she is. She could have other moms on and teach them how to derail their kids' unsuitable relationships. She's a master at it, Brant, and you don't even see it."

"No, she isn't, and she doesn't have to be. You made it easy and walked out when she asked."

"This is my fault? After all I did last night, this is my fault? Are you kidding me?"

"You didn't have to leave, Lark."

My mind spins at his audacity. And what did I expect? I just ratted out his mother, and trashed her. What was I thinking? I change the subject so

I don't do it again. "Who is Monique?"

"My old pen pal. I hadn't even met her before last night. We started writing when I was in French class in high school."

"You told me you took Spanish!" I say, remembering his explanation for knowing all of La Bamba.

"I took both. She and Mom have kept in touch and become friends. Monique came to visit Mom, and they decided to surprise me."

"Oh, so there's a shocker. Your mom approves of you spending time with Monique."

"Uh huh."

"Her disapproval of me was very clear, did I mention that?"

"You still shouldn't have left."

"I knew this would happen. I'd let you anywhere near my heart, and your mom shows up with a frown and I'd regret letting you in."

"That's your fault, Lark. If I'd been there to stand up for you, I would have. But she just has to drop in and ask politely for you to leave and you do? What's with that? Aren't I worth more to you than that? I didn't know you were such a pushover."

The words feel like a slap, a hard slap across my face. What doesn't he get? I tried everything I knew to show him how worth it he is to me, and he calls me a...a pushover?

"Your problem is, you don't let people in. These last weeks you let me get close and see who you really are. But the first obstacle that comes our way and you're out the door. I guess that's better to know now than later."

"I let people in."

"No, you don't. You don't even let your mother get close to you."

"I went out with a friend last night." I'm guiding the subject away from Mama, since he's right. Some of his remarks have hit close inside and left marks and bruises to be thought over later.

"Good. Maybe you can call her every time something comes up that sends you running."

The bruises hurt. The words ache inside, echoing inside, with the image of his angry face still so fresh in my mind. I want to get away and nurse these unfamiliar injuries in private.

I cross the street, leaving the last two red cannas on the ground,

LARKSPUR

unplanted, to die.

I explore the therapeutic powers found in mint-chocolate-chip ice cream, and although I don't feel any better afterwards, I am impressed that I managed to eat an entire pint. Actually, I feel kind of sick, but my extreme ice cream overdose assures me that the pain that is Brant is truly a new one for me.

It shouldn't be too much to want a guy who can say, "Hey, Mom, good to see you, but I had plans with my girlfriend." I mean, is that asking so much?

Deciding I don't want to be home should Brant come apologize (and he should!), I go for a walk. I don't know where I've been lately, or maybe it happened overnight or something, but there are wild flamingoes everywhere. Lots of businesses have them, I notice. Some of the flamingoes are pretty, and others are funny, but they're all unique.

I kick rocks and pout, and hope I'm walking off all that mint-chocolate-chip ice cream. When I realize the sun is setting, I rush home. Thinking I have enough time to make it to the lake, I get in my car and make it just as the sun's orange bottom touches the horizon ahead of me. Exhaling deeply as I sit at the end of the pier, it feels like some sort of victory to have made it here, at just the right moment. The fish jump, and the water laps against the pier, and I am mesmerized by the beauty of the scene God has placed before me. For once, I am not so caught up in the details of life to miss this, and that is truly something to be grateful for.

I don't check my cell phone for messages or my email when I get home. Not because I don't want to know if there is a message waiting, but because I am certain that if there isn't, my newfound, fragile peace will shatter. In order to protect it a little longer, I head to Mama's. It's a little later than I usually drop in on her, but it's been a long time with the new job and all.

I run into Stanley, who is coming out the front door with a small suitcase. His face looks drawn, older.

"Stanley? Is everything okay?"

"Yeah, just taking your mom some things. She's doing better today."

"What do you mean? Where's Mama?" I close the gap between us quickly, trying to will him to speak faster, to answer my questions.

"She's in the hospital. Didn't...? Oh, I'm sorry, Lark. I thought Mrs. Wills was going to call you. She must have told me to do that, and I got confused. Gracie's all right. She had a heart attack last night, but she's doing better today. Really."

I feel stupid for sitting on a pier and watching a sunset trying to not obsess about mint chocolate calories and a new boyfriend's mother. How shallow can I be? My own mom is lying in a hospital and I didn't even know. I hurry Stanley into my car and drive as fast as I can, not caring if Tom or any other officer has a problem with my speed. After all, I have some time to make up for.

Stanley fills me in on the details while we drive, Stanley-style, which is infuriating. I pry each bit of information out of him with three questions per full detail. She felt weird last night, like her chest hurt, and she had some numbness. She laid down for a while to rest, but after 45 minutes still felt bad. So when she also felt nauseous, they went to the hospital, which was good to have caught it so quickly. Now they needed to decide the best treatment option for her. I feel like I'm the one who survived a heart attack by the time I get us to the hospital, but I feel bad for Stanley, who is pale and has dirty, haven't-had-a-shower-in-a-day hair.

It's well after dark by the time we get there, and the brightness of the fluorescent lights glare, making the hard surfaces seem harder, and the expressions on the faces less friendly.

A cut-glass vase of yellow daisies adorns a nurses' station, but they're wilting, and the water needs to be changed. I look away, reminding myself that the flowers are neglected because the nurses are too busy taking care of patients, not because they can't keep a simple bunch of daisies healthy. It's still not an inspiring thought.

Stanley nods, almost imperceptibly, to a nurse coming out of Mama's room, and we go in wordlessly. I'm not prepared for the hospital version of my usually vibrant Mama. She's half sitting and has various machines hooked up to her, monitoring who knows what. They hum around her, but her eyes are closed; I can't tell if she's praying or sleeping. Stanley nods at me, then at the empty chair next to her bed, so I sit.

Her face is turned toward me, and her mouth open just a little, and I focus on her every breath. Finally deciding she is sleeping, I curl up in the

LARKSPUR

chair and pray silently. I wake with a start, instantly guilty that I fell asleep at all. I'd meant to pray all night, somehow making up for my absence when Mama needed me the most. It's in the middle of the night, and a nurse comes in to check on her. She's young, with red hair, and I wonder if she knows what she's doing.

Mama doesn't awaken, and the nurse writes in a file. "Are you her daughter?"

"Yes," I whisper back.

"She mentioned you last night. You from out of town?"

"No, no, I just found out." A fresh wave of guilt washes over me again. "I-I got here as soon as I found out."

"That's nice. I'm sure it means a lot to her." The nurse smiles at me and slips out the door. When she's careful not to let it shut too loudly, I decide she must be competent after all.

Stanley is reading a hunting magazine in the corner. I didn't know he hunted, and it reminds me of Elmer Fudd. He doesn't seem the type, but I guess I wouldn't know.

"Hi." Mama's voice cracks, and I jump, not having realized she was awake. Stanley and I move closer, and I take her right hand in mine. It's limp, and I've never seen her so—lifeless. A lump rises in my throat at this thought, but I smile anyway.

"Hi, Mama. I'm sorry it took me so long. How are you?"

"Fine, don't worry. Just tired." She takes in a jagged breath. "I'll be fine, baby." Her eyelids close twice while she's speaking, and I squeeze her hand so she won't feel like she has to talk any longer.

Stanley kisses her forehead and dims the light he was using in the corner. He nods toward the door, and we go into the glare of the fluorescently lit hall. We stand there, blinking, and he convinces me to go home. "Really, Lark. I'll call you tomorrow, and you can call me to find out how she is—around the clock. But go get some sleep."

I don't ever remember hugging Stanley before, but I do now. His arms stay at his sides and he seems uncomfortable. Or angry. I don't know which, since it's Stanley, and all. Feeling stupid, I leave, and the halls seem even brighter now because of the tears in my eyes.

17

I cannot recall how many times I have brushed off Brant in the last two weeks. Four, maybe five? The last time we spoke I at least had the sense to explain what had happened with Mama, and that my attention was all hers at the moment.

He sounded hurt, but what does he expect? As if Mama's recovery isn't hard enough, I'm realizing just how much Mama didn't tell me. Like about the symptoms that led to this whole thing in the first place. She was even on medication, not that she bothered to mention it to me. So I'm making sure I'm around all the time now. If Mama has something going on, I'll be there to notice, whether she feels like sharing it or not. I always thought we were closer than that, but I guess not.

Stanley has been distant, too, in his Stanley way. He glances at me from the corner of his eye sometimes when I ask too many questions, or when he thinks I should leave when she's tired. One day he told me that Mama didn't need me there to watch her sleep and would rest better if I wasn't looking at her so closely. And Stanley won't explain all the arts and crafts supplies that were scattered all over their living room the first day Mama came home from the hospital.

He just dismissed them, despite the obvious need for an explanation of so much stuff, and said, "If she didn't tell you about this, I'm not going to now. And don't ask her anytime soon, please."

There were dozens of bags of feathers, strands of beads, glue guns, assorted miniature pom poms, and so much more, and I'm not supposed to ask why? Fine. This role of prodigal daughter really stinks, especially since I didn't even realize the prodigal part applied until too late.

So one night after again overstaying my welcome, I go to Java, The Hut to find comfort in biscotti and three café mochas. I don't know why anyone actually eats those hard-as-a-brick biscotti things, but I remember this too late and buy one anyway. It doesn't help, and neither does the sight of Brant's mother as I leave. I'm almost to my car, and three cars over is Mrs. Stephens.

She's appropriately bunned and silk pantsuited as usual, and she's standing next to Brant. They have their backs to me, and they're talking and laughing with a pretty brunette. I'm glad it's not Monique, but who is this girl? And what is Mrs. Stephens doing back in town so soon?

"Thanks for dinner, Brant," the brunette says with a coy sideways look. Seriously, it was coy, and I can see it from here.

"You're welcome, it was nice. I'll call you tomorrow, Mom."

And then, *in front of his mother*—can you believe the nerve?—she leans over and kisses his cheek! What a tramp. Total tramp. My fists ball at my sides, but Mrs. Stephens and the tramp are about to leave, and I have to decide right at that moment if I'm going to watch in furious silence or if I'm going to go make a scene. I choose wrongly, of course.

"Hi, Brant! Nice to see you, Mrs. Stephens." I come over, and mother and son both look surprised and a tad apprehensive. I stick my hand out, unballed at last, and offer it to the tramp to shake. "I'm Lark."

She does one of those limp, pathetic handshakes. I hate those. "Hi, I'm Elaine."

"I don't usually do this, but let me show you something, Elaine." I smile at her to mask my disdain.

But anyone who isn't too timid to kiss someone else's boyfriend in front of his mother is surely not too timid to properly shake hands. I take her hand and demonstrate a firm handshake. "That's how you do that, even if you're shaking hands with a woman. No one likes a limp handshake."

I smile because Elaine looks petrified. Maybe I'm talking a little too loudly, now that I think about it. Maybe I shook her hand with a little bit of my bone-crushing fury, but I'm sure she got the point. "It just seems…weak."

"Thank you," she says and takes back her hand with enough force to make me think she's definitely not weak.

"Larkspuuur, how interesting to see you pop up here and stage an impromptu lesson on etiquette…of all things." Mrs. Stephens says, with a sweeping look at my wrinkled wannabe nurse attire.

"Yes, well, I think I'm done." I look to Brant, who has said nothing at all. When his mouth remains closed, I turn and leave without good-bye. I thought I would have ended this by sailing into that scene and maybe Brant would have introduced me or something. But instead, I'm leaving and they're all still there, as if I'm the one who didn't belong, instead of the tramp with the timid handshake.

But I'm too tired for this, so I drive home. Timid, wimpy tears slip down my cheeks because no one noticed I was the one who should have been there, not Elaine.

My phone doesn't ring. I take a bath with my favorite—spring green Vitabath bubble bath—and paint my toenails Passion Pink. But I forget that I can't get out of the tub with wet toenails without submerging them in the water, so I wait forever for my slow drain to empty the water. By the time I'm out of what was supposed to be a hot, relaxing bath, I'm freezing again. I crawl into bed, while brushing my teeth, and start my laptop so I can check email.

Four messages from andiloveher! Four, in the last week, and I guess I haven't been checking, even at work when it would have been so easy.

I start with the oldest, and end with the most recent.

Lark, let me know when you have time to see me. Even if it's just a sunset or a coffee.

The next one, sent the next day, simply said:

Or a popsicle.

The third one reads:

I hate how we left things and I miss you. Could you at least tell me if you're still interested in dating me?

Major guilt pangs there.
The last one, dated yesterday:

LARKSPUR

Lark, my mother is coming into town with another "friend." I'd love for you to join us for dinner if you can spare the time. Tell your mother hello, please.

Major, major guilt pangs. He invited me! But why doesn't he just tell his mom to quit trying to set him up? Why do I have to join him for these awkward little get-togethers? Isn't there a better answer more in keeping with the whole "leave and cleave" philosophy?

I write to andiloveher:

Brant, just read your emails tonight. Mama is doing better, but recovery is painful. What's with all the "friends" your mom is bringing your way, and are they all kissing you?

It probably isn't the best email to send, especially after my etiquette lesson, but I hit *Send* anyway, because that's the kind of shortsighted thing I do.

~

My heart leaps at the email on my screen at work. Andiloveher writes:

Yeah, they kiss me, and give me the worst handshakes ever. Someone should really teach them how to do it right. Mom's calling these friends "traveling companions." It's okay. I know what she's doing and it's harmless. I can handle it, so don't worry about it. You're busy taking care of Mama, and that's more important than the latest tricks my mother is pulling. Miss you, and wish I were kissing you.
   Love,
   Brant

Did you get that? The second to last word is actually *love*. I obsess over whether that means he loves me, decide it must, and call in Brenda for a second opinion.

"Maybe it does mean that, Lark. But maybe it's just the way he ends emails."

She's baiting me, but I don't see it until too late.

"Does not! Never has before!"

"Would you like a daisy, and you can play the He loves me, he loves me not game and find out for sure?"

"Oh you're so funny."

"No, really." Brenda leans over, types a web address, and a screen-size daisy shows up. I click each petal and a tinny voice says, "He loves me!" with great enthusiasm, and "He loves me... not!" with great despair.

And the daisy settles it. He totally loves me.

"Ha!"

Brenda stops halfway down the hall and says, "That's the beauty of that site! He always loves you!"

"Oh. I so don't care." Oh, but I do. And I wonder how to reply to this new, affectionate, loving email. I rearrange files, then come back to it, reread, and think. (Note: I do not simply jot something off and hit *Send*, as is my custom. This is too big for that.)

After lunch, and several rereadings, I compose what I hope sounds off the top of my head. It's thought out down to the word, but hopefully that doesn't show.

> Brant,
> Miss you and miss kissing you too. Can I see you sometime this week? Will gladly furnish popsicles, and no mention of either of our mothers.
> Love,
> Lark

I delete the "love," and retype it three times. Then I type it over and over after my name. Just to see what it looks like. Really, my stomach thrills at the sight of it, and I'm experimenting with the sweet torture of immature adrenaline rushes at the sight of the typed words. It's dumb, and I feel dumb, but then Brenda comes around the corner and I didn't hear her. I grab the mouse and try to turn off the monitor but I hit *Send* and my stupid email goes off like this, instead.

LARKSPUR

Brant,

Miss you and miss kissing you too. Can I see you sometime this week? Will gladly furnish popsicles, and no mention of either of our mothers.

Love, Love, Love, Lark Love Love Love Love Love Love Love Love Love Love Love Love Love Love Love

"Noooo!" Oh my gosh, I am such a dork. So much for taking all morning to plan the perfect email! And why, after all these years, has no one invented a *Retract Send* feature? I mean, how useful would it be if you could take back accidentally sent emails?

"You know, you could call him and tell him to delete it without opening it."

"If someone you were dating did that, would you actually delete it, or would you analyze it that much more closely?"

"Yeah, I see your point. Like when you have a big zit and you do your hair really wild so no one will notice the zit, but you've only managed to call attention to it, instead of away from it."

"I've never done that."

"Oh. Yeah, me neither. Hey, have you seen the paper? There's an article on the Mystery Flamingoes."

"Mystery what?"

"You know, the flamingoes that have been popping up everywhere. We have one you walk by every day in case you haven't noticed."

"I had noticed, but I didn't know there was anything mysterious about it."

"Well there is. I have to get ready for my next class, but you should read it. I had no idea we should be so honored by that bird!"

I get the paper from the lobby and flip to the Metro section. Several small photos show close-ups of the flamingoes in front of various businesses around town. The flamingo at the courthouse appeared after the city council approved an increased awareness program for the location of sex offenders, and the flamingo bore a letter applauding the move. Signed, Supportive Citizen.

The small nondenominational church on the outskirts of town received their flamingo when they began their ministry to the women working in the "gentlemen's clubs." The letter that accompanied that bird (who wore fishnet stockings over pink stuffed legs, and a turquoise feather boa) voiced support for the move to show Christ's love to these women, often overlooked by ministries.

I run down the hall to where Brenda is sitting. Apparently class prep time involves brushing her hair. "Hey, what did the Arts Center do to get a bird?"

These flamingoes have Mama's style all over them, and the art supplies I saw in her living room. I'm half afraid that the letter accompanying the Arts Center flamingo says, "Thanks for hiring my kid."

"We got it when we started helping the after-school program with the at-risk kids. Their classes are free, you know."

"Oh, right."

So relieved. And shocked to learn that it's Mama who is the anonymous Plains Point citizen whose opinions have become greatly noticeable. Businesses proudly display their birds as a local sign of community success. They've somehow become a coveted stamp of approval.

And I didn't know about this *how?* I thought Mama and I were so much closer than we are, and it hurts to think that she's the town's secret bird-giver, and not even I knew it. And why not? It's not like I would tell anyone. Really. I wouldn't. I'd scout for worthy recipients and discreetly tell her of my findings, but that's it.

The other thing that's funny is that the birds arrive in the night, with a letter explaining why it has been given. I get a kick out of Mama running clandestine errands to deliver wildly attired flamingoes, all under cover of darkness, and in the name of good. And I can't believe I didn't think of her—I mean, only Mama would dream up Mystery Flamingoes.

I stop by an art supply store after work, picking up anything bright and outlandish and Mama-ish. I figure she needs the stuff, and it would be good to help her get into something again besides focusing so much on her slow recovery.

She's recuperating well, but a few new supplies will surely help. And really, if I'm honest, I'd like her to tell me about the Mystery Flamingoes herself.

I push open the door with my shoulder, as is my habit recently, so Mama doesn't have to get up. She's sitting on the couch, with her feet on a tufted ottoman in front of her and a book she puts down when I come in.

"Hi, how ya feeling today?"

"Better. What's all that?"

Setting the bags next to her on the couch, I say, "Bright feathers, strands of beads, sequins, fake flowers, anything you might need or want."

"Need or want for what?"

"Need or want for, um, your flamingoes. You're the one who makes them, aren't you?"

"Yes. And I didn't need any of this." Her face, usually relaxed and friendly, looks creased and angry. "Who have you told?"

"No one!" I'm hurt at her expression. She really didn't want me to know. And why did that escape me? "Mama, why didn't you want me to know?"

"Why should you, Lark? What do you really know about me anyway?"

"What?" It must be the medication. What do I really know about her anyway?

"Do you know anything about my husband and my marriage and my health and this thing with the birds?" She points toward the flamingo peeking from behind the couch. I hadn't noticed it before. "If I'd died, would you even really know me?"

That's what this is about, but I don't deal with that last question. Can't begin to imagine how, actually. "How could I ask you about your health and flamingoes if I don't know there are health issues and birds to ask about in the first place?"

"It's fine. You keep everyone at bay, Lark, always have. And then when someone does the same thing, you don't like it."

Mama has never, never spoken to me like this before. It feels like a punch to the stomach, so painful is the force of her words.

"Well, why?"

"Why? Because you're not interested in me as a person. You're interested in me as Mama, so I've been that for you. And my projects and health and husband don't have anything to do with the part of me you care about."

I hate it that she's right. My own self-centeredness is a nasty thing, staring back at me in memories, now apparent for the first time. The time Stanley mentioned Mama's special "ministry" to the city, when we were having lunch somewhere, and she actually blushed. How was it that I didn't ask? It didn't seem important to me then somehow. And I'd seen her taking medication—had I asked her what the pills were for—even once? I'd assumed they were for a headache she hadn't mentioned, but I should have known. It's not like she was trying to keep it from me. I had no idea I could be so selfish and so uncaring toward the person who has meant so much to me.

But she's right. At the hospital right before she was released, she asked me who I was dating. And did I tell her, eager to let her in, and distract her from the pain she was in? No. I'd changed the subject, and never did tell her. I've been so annoyed about how Brant has handled his mom, and never stopped and wondered how he feels about my not even telling mine. That can't feel great either.

I'm suddenly tired, worn out by the weight of the realization of my own ickiness. My own ability to so easily hurt the people I love. I gently give Mama a hug, which she halfheartedly returns. I ask if she needs anything, and when she doesn't, I gladly leave.

Eager to be alone to search my heart for more evidence of selfishness, I get a café mocha and head for the upcoming sunset. This is a sort of honest wallowing that can't be done in a room with striped walls that can make you dizzy. This can only be done in the reflected brightness of the sun on the water.

18

Brenda plops down in the chair across from my desk, eating a granola bar. It looks especially unappetizing. We've gotten in the habit of eating lunch this way most days, across my desk and giggling over the latest things that her students have said.

Brenda leans over and whispers, "There is a rumor going around that Sasha is quitting soon."

"Really?" Sasha is the bookkeeper, and I've secretly coveted her job since my arrival. How Brenda knows this is beyond me, because I really thought I'd done a good job of keeping my covetousness under wraps.

"Yep. You know you're qualified. Keep an eye on it. It pays way more than what you make."

"Huh." It feels wrong to be whispering about a not yet vacated job, so I change the subject. "What did you wear when Carl proposed?"

Brenda pops the last bite of granola bar in her mouth and brushes the crumbs to the carpet while she thinks. "Old jeans and a stained Audio Adrenaline T-shirt."

"Nooo!"

"Yeah. We'd been volunteering at the homeless shelter, making sandwiches. We hadn't planned to, but our Sunday school class signed up, and then a bunch of people forgot. So we went, and he proposed afterwards in the park over on Avenue H."

The park on Avenue H is probably the single most unromantic place I can think of. The swings are broken and the merry-go-round dips so sharply on one side that it barely moves anymore. An old stained T-shirt would fit in there, but a marriage proposal? Maybe she didn't expect it, and therefore could not dress for the occasion.

"Did you know it was coming?"

"Sure." She narrows her eyes at me. "Is Brant close to asking you?"

"Nope. I was wondering what to wear, anyway."

"Depends on if you're serving sandwiches to the homeless."

"I was more concerned with looking good, rather than being virtuous."

"Uh huh, I got that. You still hung up on the whole boob thing?"

I so resent that question and do not admire Brenda's directness just now. "Maybe. But really, can you not put it that way? Sounds gross."

I don't think she's listening to me anyway. "Why is it we always want what we don't have?" she asks. "I used to obsess about pierced ears, until I got them. Then it was blond highlights. Boy, that was a mistake. You know, you'd probably be griping about your butt if it wasn't so great, too."

"Yathink?" When I can't mentally picture my own butt, I stand and try to turn to look at it. That never works, by the way.

"Oh yeah. Beyonce would trade butts with you any day."

"Beyonce?"

"You know, she even has her own butt dance."

"No...really? I'm not picturing this." I'm speaking slowly, as if trying to recall what Brenda is referring to, and she falls for it.

Brenda stands, looks around for anyone, and when the coast is clear, assumes a really awkward position. She has her arms in front of her, chest height, and bent at the elbows. Then she starts doing this horrendous butt shaking, up and down movement that looks more like a seizure than a dance.

Tears roll down my face, and my cheeks hurt from laughing, so awful is this impersonation.

She stops, and asks, "Now do you know who I mean?"

"Oh, Brenda, I knew who you meant." I wipe away a tear. "I just wanted to see if you'd do that!"

"Lark!" She's outraged, or pretending to be.

"That was *painful* looking, Brenda. Promise me you'll never do that in public again."

"Come on." She motions for me to get up and follow her, and I do, although I'm not sure where she's going to take me or what she's going to do to me. "I've wanted to do this for a few days, but now you don't have a choice. You made me booty dance for no reason."

LARKSPUR

We slip into the prop room, where all kinds of costumes are stored, and Brenda shuts the door behind me.

"Pick a wig. The nicer ones are over there." And she points to the mirrored dressing table, which has several of the better looking ones on white Styrofoam heads.

I select the most Julia Roberts-ish one, and hold it up for Brenda's approval.

"Good. Now take this." Brenda tosses me one of the most amazingly bad bras I've ever seen. It's neon purple and has giant molded, stand alone, no boobs required cups. I catch it, but only from instinct since it's flying across the room at me, not because I want to touch the thing.

"That is not just a bra. That is what you call a 'brassiere.'"

"No kidding, it's actually *heavy*. And I am not putting it on."

"Oh, yes you are, Lark. I booty danced. You're putting that on. Now go." Brenda motions to the dressing room behind me, and I go. At least the giant purple brassiere looks clean.

There isn't a mirror in the dressing room, so I put it on, put on my shirt and then the wig and come out.

"This feels so wrong. I mean, how enormous are these things?" My silhouette is so changed, it's like I am suddenly an alien. Or Pamela Anderson, with Julia Roberts' hair.

"You know, those aren't that big. It just seems like it to you because you're not used to it. Go ahead, look." Brenda points to the mirror. "Like it?"

"Not even a little. I look like Mr. Incredible."

Brenda gives me a blank look.

"You know, that animated movie *The Incredibles*? The dad was huge on top and skinny on bottom."

"He had breasts?"

"No, that's not what I meant."

"So why don't you like this look?" Brenda asks in her best Dr. Phil voice.

"I look like a freak."

"Nope. You don't. The hair is realistic, and no one would know that's a massive purple brassiere in there."

I look again, and she's right. It's not that it looks like a bad costume. It just doesn't look right at all.

"Okay, I get your point. I'm returning to normal, now, never to wish for these—" I point to my chest—"again."

I'm almost dressed when Brenda calls out, "You know what you put in brassieres?"

"What?"

"Bosoms!" She cracks up, and I come out, transformed to my normal self. "I've always hated that word!"

"Yeah, me too."

We return to my desk, where Brenda whispers, "You had big purple *bosoms* in a *brassiere!*"

"Yes, I did. And you booty danced like a dying animal," I whisper back.

"Yes, I did."

⁂

"I shouldn't be here," I tell Brenda. We're sitting in a dimly lit Italian restaurant I've never been to before, waiting for her cousin to join us.

"What were you going to do instead? Beat yourself up over the thing with your mother, stay home and obsess over your appearance, or agonize over why Brant hasn't returned your calls in the last couple of days?"

"All three."

"Right. So instead you're here with me. Hey, I don't want to be here either, but Carl is out of town."

"What? Did I hear you right?"

"No offense." She's stammering, and the lights are too low to tell for sure, but I think she might be blushing. "I just mean, I'd rather be with him since I'm, um, ovulating...and we're *trying*—"

I am uncomfortable with the word *ovulating* entering this conversation, but I pretend otherwise. "Are you really? That's great!"

"But since he's out of town, I'm here with you. My cousin is never in town and specifically asked if I had any cute friends."

"He didn't!" Brenda knows I wouldn't be sitting here if she'd told me this before.

She nods.

"I have a boyfriend."

"One you're not completely happy with, one who isn't returning your calls, and one whose mother despises your existence."

"So?" It comes out as lame as that, too. But really? Things with Brant have gotten so hopeless that Brenda is trying to set me up with people now?

I brace myself against the cute man vibes, since I'm so weak in that area, and it's a good thing, because a really cute one is heading our way. With two bouquets of wilted flowers that probably came from a supermarket. How sweet is that? Cute and bearing flowers…I will not be tempted.

Oddly, I'm not. Hank is great, and yes, that's really his name. He's an engineer and has loads of charm to go with those flowers, but I'm thinking of Brant and why I couldn't be wherever he is tonight.

"So, Lark, you work at the Arts Center, too?"

"Yeah, but I'm not really artistic like Brenda. I just coordinate the classes."

"You should see her walls; she's definitely artistic."

Okay, shut up, Brenda. We do not want to invite your cousin to see my apartment.

Hank leans across the table, tents his fingers beneath his chin, and studies me. I stop myself from blurting out that I have a boyfriend, and he should really be looking at someone else that way. Not because I don't want to say that, but because it occurs to me that he might not be thinking along those lines at all, and then I'd look like a big, vain idiot. I decide I will work in the "boyfriend" detail into conversation as soon as possible, rather than declaring it.

Brenda's cell phone rings and she answers it with an apologetic look to both of us.

"Really? How soon?" She's showing much more interest in this conversation than she has in the one with her long-lost cousin.

Please, God, don't let her bail on me.

"Okay, I'll meet you there! This could be it!" I'm already glaring at her when she hangs up, but she doesn't notice. Or at least she pretends not to notice, I'm not sure which. And how ugly of me anyway, to try to deny my married friend the um, joy of wedded bliss, in the name of future children. I'll probably look into their cherubic faces one day and remember how selfish I was tonight, and that it could have prevented their existence.

"So, I'm going to go, and I'm glad you two are getting along. Lark, would you tell Hank why this is so important for me? Thanks!" And she kisses the top of his head, waves at me, and flies out of the restaurant with her bouquet of wilting flowers in one hand and her car keys jingling in the other.

"Uh," I start, but how do you tell a guy that his cousin is ovulating? I mean, gross. "Brenda, um, and Carl, are trying to...start their family." I look at Hank to see if this is enough, and I shouldn't have worried. Hank, being a guy and all, gets my reference to sex without further explanation. Should have known.

"Oh! Like, right *now*."

"Seems that way." I shift in my seat, completely uncomfortable with discussing Brenda's sex life.

"So, do you want kids?"

I mentally, silently scream. "Um, one day. You?"

"Oh yeah. My girlfriend wants three, and I think that's a good number."

"Your...your girlfriend?" I'm so glad I didn't open my mouth and reveal my big, vain idiotic self. But why did he ask if Brenda had any cute friends?

"Her name is Josie. Honestly, I'm thinking of proposing, but I wanted to go out with a lot of nice women first, just to be sure I'm doing the right thing."

"That's an interesting approach to 'doing the right thing.'"

"Oh, she knows. She said if I need to make sure she's the one I want to be with forever, and that's how I need to do it, she's okay with that."

"How's it gone?"

"Great. You know, I'm seeing all these gorgeous, interesting women—like you, and I'm not interested at all."

LARKSPUR

The waiter places a plate in front of me, and I don't think it's what I ordered, but I don't care. I'm that eager for a distraction from being told I'm not in the least bit of a temptation to the opposite sex. Really, why not eat some other person's pasta, when it can help you avoid the realization that you're unappealing?

Hank goes on, oblivious to his insult. "Lark, it's like this. How great is it that I can be here with you and know that I don't need to date any other women. I've found her. I just need to give her the ring, get on my knee, and ask her. I'm so excited to know that."

"That's great, Hank." And I actually mean it, because he has found his Josie. "I have a boyfriend, anyway, Hank. He isn't returning my calls right now, but maybe one day I'll have a boyfriend who thinks that way about me."

"You will, Lark." He grabs my hand and squeezes it. I think he does this more because he's excited at his own realization of his consuming love for Josie, but I can't be sure.

"Larkspuuur!"

I jump, dropping my fork, which clatters on the edge of my plate before falling to the floor. I know the voice instantly, and it belongs to the last person I want to see after having already been declared undesirable, and dumped by my friend due to her ovulatory cycle.

Mrs. Stephens, teal silk pantsuit and chignon, stands next to me, with a smile that is triumphant if not friendly.

"Hi, Mrs. Stephens."

"Aren't you going to introduce me to your handsome friend?"

"Certainly, Mrs. Stephens, this is Hank." I don't know Hank's last name, so I leave it at that. I'm already picturing how quickly she might tell Brant of my dining with the handsome Hank. Then I laugh, nervously, because there used to be a gas station near my house called Handsome Hank's and I used to think the mustached guy on the sign really was quite handsome.

Hank shakes her hand and says something I don't catch because I'm busy being a moron.

"Is something funny, Larkspuuur, dear?" She asks it in exactly the way all teachers know how to ask that question when what they really are saying is, "Stop disturbing my class or I'll embarrass you further." I always hated it when teachers did that.

"Not really. How's Brant?"

"He's fine. As you can tell." She looks over her right shoulder at where Brant and a redhead are seated, deep in conversation. His back is to me, but I can tell he's laughing at something she's saying and leaning across the table to hear what it is. The redhead flips her hair and I recognize Danica. My stomach twists in a knot. "Nice to see you," she says, smiling at me, and goes back to the table to join Brant and Danica.

"Who was that?" Hank asks, popping a bite of garlic bread into his mouth.

"My boyfriend's mother. She hates me. And that's him over there, with the pretty redhead."

"Huh. She *is* pret—sorry." Hank takes another bite, then says, "Hey, maybe he's doing the same thing with her that I'm doing with you."

I try to smile but can't. Hank's attempt at kindness is no match for the knots in my stomach.

We eat quickly. Making small talk is harder than it was before Mrs. Stephens' visit. I'm relieved to see the waiter coming back with the ticket, so we can leave.

Right behind the waiter is Mrs. Stephens, though, followed by Brant and Danica. Mrs. Stephens doesn't stop, at least, but she does give me a smirk as she passes. When she passes our table, Brant looks up and sees me. He opens his mouth to say hi, but then his eyes travel to Hank. Then to the flowers, and back to me. He shakes his head slightly, and I open my mouth to say something, but nothing comes out. Before I know it, they're gone, and I'm left with Handsome Hank, wilted flowers, and the sinking understanding that Brant has gotten the wrong idea completely.

"Hey, Lark," Hank says to me, and I look at him. "I, uh, think he got the wrong idea about us, but face it. He was here with another girl, too."

I don't tell him that it isn't the same thing at all—that Brant and his mother go on dates with other women frequently. I mean, that wouldn't exactly sound right, so I simply nod.

LARKSPUR

"Mama, are you busy today?"

"Nope."

"Can I come over and paint your toenails and hang out for the morning?"

"If that's what you want."

I hear the challenge in her voice. "It is what I want. Is there anything you want me to bring?"

"A Diet Coke. I'm out."

"See you soon."

I'm nervous. In my mind this is the first adult-to-adult time I'll have with Mama. I'd never noticed that it wasn't that way before, but now that she's pointed it out, the pressure is on to make this morning different. I have no idea how to do that, and I wonder if nail polish and Diet Coke are the right props. I send up prayers all the way over and knock before walking in.

I greet her the same way, put a Diet Coke on ice, and set up my pedicure station in the middle of the coffee table.

"What color is that?"

I proudly hold up the bottle. "Bought it just for this. Flamingo Pink!"

"Nice, Lark."

"I've been wondering. I always thought you and Stanley met at church, but I never asked you how."

"We didn't meet at church."

"Oh. Where'd you meet?"

"Guess."

"Through friends?"

"No."

"Supermarket?"

"Stanley doesn't go to the supermarket if he can help it."

"I don't know! Coffee shop?"

She smiles at me, savoring this for some reason, and I laugh at her. She's been more guarded lately, and I sense that she's holding onto the last bit of reserve, but maybe I'm breaking through it.

"When you were busy with all the events of a high school senior, I realized I was about to be alone. I didn't like that realization at all."

I stop painting and ask, "So what did you do about it?"

"I went to the mall and I had one of those glamour photographers dress me up like some sort of madam and take my picture. Then I plastered it on two different dating websites."

"Noooo! You did not!"

"I did." She smiles, enjoying my reaction. "It was a wonder my picture didn't scare him off. The lady at the studio put me in kelly green eye shadow and I looked like a plus-sized ice skater."

"And you never told me!"

"Nope. Never did. Not the kind of thing I would have wanted you doing, baby." She leans forward to admire my handiwork with Flamingo Pink. "*And* you didn't ask."

"Wow. What did the ad say?"

"Large, lovely, Christian woman who has to be met to be believed."

"That's true. You do have to be met to be believed. You know, Mama, I'd like to get to know Stanley, if you don't think it's too late."

"Sure. He's in the backyard. Go ask him if you can go shooting with him tomorrow after church."

"*Shooting?*"

But she only raises her eyebrows in silent challenge, so I go.

Stanley is reading the newspaper while sitting in a folding lawn chair.

"Stanley? Um, could I go shooting with you tomorrow?"

He puts down the paper and nods slowly. "Reckon that'd be okay." Stanley is a man of few words, but one of them is often *reckon*. "My friend Earle said I could use his land outside of town. I'll be leaving about three."

"Great. See you then."

He returns to his paper, and I to Mama's toenails, refusing to start getting nervous about shooting with Stanley. That can wait until later at least.

"I'll be shooting tomorrow," I tell Mama, with more brightness than I feel.

"Good. It's just pigeons you know."

"Pigeons? I didn't know we had pigeons here, or that people actually *shot* them." I stop myself from adding, "*Gross!*"

"Oh, yeah, baby. People shoot them. I've done it. It's fun."

LARKSPUR

"Really?" I so cannot picture my mother with a gun shooting at birds. "Do you eat them?"

She smiles. "No. Not too tasty. Even when I'm the chef. So, tell me about your love life."

I tell her all about Brant, about Mrs. Stephens, and about her "traveling companions."

And Mama, without me even asking, tells me all about the flamingoes, which I was hoping she'd do!

"So there you have it. It's my way of anonymously impacting this city. Much more powerful that way. The mayor wouldn't pose for a photo with a flamingo sent to him by Grace Andrews, but the mystery of it makes it seem more important."

"It *is* important, Mama."

"I know. I'm glad you think so, too."

19

Sweat is pouring down the back of my shirt, and my legs stick to the blue, cracked vinyl seats of Stanley's Ford. It is Texas Hot, as Mama sometimes says, and that's even hotter in an un-air-conditioned Ford in the middle of the afternoon. My stomach knots as we jolt along the dirt road, the truck's numerous squeaks and rattles incessant.

I sneak a peek at Stanley, who is as laid-back as ever with one arm resting on the open window and the other hand loosely holding the weathered blue steering wheel. He's in a standard-issue, old-man, one-piece, belted jumpsuit. He catches me looking and gives a small nod. He can tell I'm nervous, probably, and maybe I'm imagining it, but I think he's enjoying it. Our guns rattle in a rack behind our heads, ready. More ready than I am.

I'd rather do anything in the world besides kill innocent birds with Elmer Fudd. But for Mama, and for Stanley, I'm here, petrified.

We get out of the truck and I dutifully look for birds, relieved not to see any.

"Um, Stanley. Do you think there will be anything to shoot?" I'm looking at the sky, trying to keep the hopeful note out of my voice.

"Pigeons?"

"Yeah, that's what Mama said we were here for, right?"

"Right." He takes the guns out of the truck, smiling now. "Reckon we'll have all we want, Lark."

Stanley hardly ever smiles, and this one makes me suspicious. "Oh. Okay. This one's my rifle?"

"Shotgun, Lark." He pulls on a dirty looking baseball hat that he had in the bed of the truck. "That's a shotgun."

He proceeds to show me how to load, hold, and aim it. His hands are steady, and I'm glad he's so patient with me. Last thing you want when you're getting a firearms lesson is an impatient stepfather. My heart is thudding anyway, but this part I can handle. It's what comes next that has me so scared. I'm remembering the passage that talks about how God knows when each sparrow falls, and figure it must be the same for pigeons.

"Here, Lark, you practice sighting over there while I get us set up." He goes to the bed of the truck, and I try to look like I'm practicing "sighting," but I have no idea if that's what I'm doing. Really, I'm praying that God makes sure Mama understands how far I am willing to go in order to know who she is.

Stanley sets up some sort of machine and weights it with an old tire. I don't even want to know what that thing does. He returns with a cardboard box, sets it down, and opens it. "Here, Lark." He hands me a circular disc from the box. It's about four inches in diameter and painted fluorescent orange with a black perimeter.

"What do I do with this?"

"That's a pigeon."

That makes no sense. It's a circle, made of who knows what. "What do you mean?"

"That's a clay *pigeon*, and we're going to shoot them." Stanley flashes me a rare smile and waits for me to understand.

"Oh!" Huge relief. Not birds. Stupid circle targets that aren't even bird shaped! "Oh, thank you, Stanley."

"No problem." I can tell now that he's been laughing at me the whole time, but I'm so glad I won't be killing that I don't even care.

Now it's clear Mama has been mad at me. She knew I thought I was murdering birds today, and she just smiled.

Stanley loads the machine with a few clay pigeons and gives me earplugs. Then I can't hear what he's saying, and he just points to the air, then to my gun, and mouths, "Shoot."

So I shoot. Despite the earplugs, the loud bang of the gun startles me. The first pigeons soar upwards into the air ahead of us about twenty feet high. I miss.

Stanley re-loads the machine with the old tire leaning on it, and I miss some more, but then I get three in a row. I stop to make sure Stanley saw.

I take out my earplugs, and he comes over to remind me to keep the butt of the gun against my shoulder so it won't slam into me each time I shoot.

We shoot for almost an hour, and only stop when the box is empty.

"Stanley! This is so much fun! I mean, I don't want to kill anything, but I think I like this!"

"Yep."

"I might need a rifle of my own—can I come back with you sometime?" We're loading things back into the bed of the Ford, and I'm so excited I feel like a yappy dog—and probably sound like one too, but I don't care.

"Shotgun, Lark. It's a shotgun." He wipes the sweat from his forehead with the dirty baseball cap. "You can come out with me anytime you want."

We drive back to town, talking about shooting. He drops me off in front of Mrs. Huttle's house. "You're a good kid, Lark."

"You're a good man, Stanley. I'm glad you and Mama found each other."

"I reckon that was God."

※

The last few days when I left messages on Brant's answering machine, I didn't really worry when he didn't call back. I mean, it's Brant, after all, and if something were wrong he'd just tell me. He's not the sort of guy to disappear like that—at least I don't think so. But since that awful dinner misunderstanding, I've left two messages and those haven't been returned either. For some reason, it feels different now. Worse. More final. More like rejection.

The slow burn of rejection turns into resentment. I can't stand Mrs. Stephens, who was so "not a factor" that she played a rather large part in why Brant and I aren't speaking. With all the ridiculous "traveling companions" in blond, brunette, and redhead varieties, and then her insults, and who knows what else she said and did that I don't know about

LARKSPUR

I was thinking about this one day when Brenda came in and reminded me it would be better to know that sort of thing now, before signing up to be her daughter-in-law. "Trust me," she'd said. "It's worse when your mother-in-law seems like a sweet, supportive person and then only turns into a dragon once you're married and you can't change your mind."

It's the first time Brenda has mentioned her mother-in-law, so I'm surprised. "I didn't know you two didn't get along."

"Oh, we did. But that was before we mentioned that we wanted to start a family soon. Then she got all weird and let it slip that she had thought we wouldn't make it long enough to raise a child together, and are we sure that's what we wanted to do right now?"

"She didn't!"

"Oh yeah. She was being nice to me because she thought I was only the *first* wife!"

"That's awful!"

"No kidding. Choose your mother-in-law as carefully as you choose a man, Lark."

I toss a dried-up jar of red paint into the trash can and wonder if Brenda would have still married Carl if she'd known the truth of what her future mother-in-law would be like. I'm almost positive she would have.

I'm still cleaning out the old paints from a supply closet when Brant comes in. I'd about given up on him, and us, so I'm surprised. He's holding a pink gerbera daisy and the look on his face is enough to make me hope that things aren't as bad as I thought.

"Hi," I say, closing the door to the supply closet.

He holds out the daisy, and when I take it, he asks if I can have lunch with him. A man bearing a single, pink daisy. As if I'd say no!

"Sure, I'll be back in a minute." I don't need to go tell anyone I'm leaving, or do anything besides pull myself together and say a prayer in the bathroom, but I excuse myself anyway.

I keep him waiting on purpose, and when I return, Brant tentatively holds out a hand to me, which I take. He holds the door open for me as we walk outside, past the flamingo standing sentry.

Brant doesn't head toward his car but leads me to a picnic set up under a tree around the side of the building that overlooks a small flower garden.

"I guess you were pretty sure I'd say yes?"

"No. But I took a chance anyway."

I have no idea what to say to him. I really don't want a boyfriend who dates every pretty girl his mother can find, and then makes excuses for it. And I don't want to defend myself for being at that restaurant with Hank. Maybe that's just me being stubborn, but since I can't think of something nice to say, I keep silent. I sit on the blanket and watch the ridiculously attired flamingo in the distance, instead of Brant.

"I'm sorry I haven't called. I got your messages the day after I saw you last, but I didn't know what to think."

"I'd been calling you for days *before* that," I say, because I don't want to admit that Hank was a misunderstanding yet. He hasn't mentioned Danica yet, after all.

"Really?" He looks surprised.

"Yes, really." I focus on the flamingo, whose argyle tie flutters in the breeze.

"My mom was staying with me then. Did you call my cell phone or my house?"

"House." I can only manage this one word without giving into the temptation to trash-talk his mother. For once, I am wise enough to clamp my mouth shut.

"I'll have to ask if she got those messages." He's been fixing plates of sandwiches and fruit and places one in front of me. "I'm sorry, Lark. I think we just figured out what happened there."

Big mystery.

"Are you seeing anyone else?"

How he thinks he has a right to ask this, I have no idea. "No. Unlike you, who date everyone pretty your mom can bring your way—with or without me knowing."

"Not anymore. I don't know why I didn't see how manipulative and weird that was, but I get it now."

I study his face, and he means what he's saying.

"I thought I was somehow honoring her by not contradicting her. Every time I brought it up before, she'd make sure I knew how much she needed me and how happy she'd be if I went out with her and her friend—whoever that was—that one more time."

"Uh huh."

"Lark, I'm sorry. She tried everything she could to ruin what we had, and I let her. But please let me make it up to you. I really want you back. I want to be spending time with you again, whether we're doing errands for your mother or painting rooms, or just jogging. I miss you."

"I want you back, too." He sees what his mom has been doing? Oh, praise God!

"I love you."

The words catch me off guard completely. "You... really?"

His dimples deepen as he smiles. "Yeah. I really do. If I were smarter, I'd have done years of my life differently, simply to have more of them with you."

He's facing me, holding my hands, and I want to say it back, but words can't pass the lump in my throat. I hope he understands.

"You're beautiful, and different, and fun, and my whole life is more—alive—with you in it. That's why these last weeks have been so rough. No one else has ever made me so glad to get up each morning."

Tears start running down my cheeks and I throw my arms around his neck since I can't seem to say anything. Instead, I kiss his hair, behind his left ear since that's what's closest, and cry.

"You okay?" Brant asks after a minute.

"Yeah." I sound like I have a bad cold, but at least my voice is working. I smile to reassure him, because he looks really worried now.

"I love you too." A loud, awful sounding sob escapes and I hug him again, but he just laughs at me. And I smile into the wet hair behind his ear, because it is startling to finally feel this sort of love—the kind I've always wondered about, prayed for, and dreamed of. To finally have it this close, all around me, like the graceful branches of a willow, embracing me right back.

"I want to share you with Mama. I want Stanley to meet you and love you."

"You want Stanley to love me?" he teases.

"Yes. I do. Stanley and Mama are more important to me now than they've ever been. More than I've ever *let* them be. So I want them to love you."

"Okay then. I hope Stanley loves me too."

But I wonder if this is going to work, even as my thoughts are racing ahead. "What would be different?" And another thought comes to mind. He hasn't even asked about Hank! Isn't he jealous? And why not? Shouldn't he be jealous?

"Everything will be different, Lark."

"Why?"

"I told my mom last night that I was going to do everything I could to get you back. That any interference in our relationship in the future would mean the end of her relationship with me."

"You said *what*?" This is more than I ever would have asked of him. I don't think that I'd ever ask him to put me that much higher above his mother—even though I'd want him to. That he did it now, not knowing if we were even dating, and without even talking to me about it first, melts the icy edge of anger I've held against him and his mother for the last weeks.

"Yes. And I mean it. You're that important to me."

We hug, and it's awkward because as much as I'd love to cling to his neck I'm trying not to lean into his plate or mine.

"One thing, though."

"Anything." And then I know what he's going to ask, and I get butterflies. He's going to ask me to disavow Handsome Hank. He wants to envision our future together and there is this one attractive engineer in the way, it seems, and he must know the truth. He is desperately in love with me and so jealous he cannot see straight.

"I'd like for you to have dinner with my mom and me tonight."

"Oh." I can't remember. Did I say "anything" out loud a second ago, when he said he wanted one thing from me? Maybe I just thought it. *Please, God, tell me I kept my mouth shut, and I really just thought it.*

"Lark. If she doesn't approve, I don't care. I won't love you less."

"Really?"

"How could I explain that I fell in love with a girl who cried when she heard Willie sing 'Pancho and Lefty'? My mom only cares about professional ambitions."

LARKSPUR

"As far as those go, I might not always be a disappointment to her." I haven't told Brant of my recent goals, and I hesitate to do so now.

"Then it might be something else that bugs her. Who cares? She's impossible to please, and you don't have to ever try to live up to what you think she wants for me."

"I didn't know you knew I cried."

"Oh yeah."

"That's such a sad song. No one heard Pancho's dying words."

He smiles at me and just says, "I know, Lark."

And the warmth returns, and I push the thought of Mrs. Stephens out of my mind for the moment. This moment is mine, and she can't have it. I smile, tip my head to the right, and flirt outrageously with this man who loves me.

"You should really kiss me."

"You're so smart."

20

I knock on Mrs. Huttle's door when I get home from work. I haven't spoken to her in a while, and I want to make sure she's okay.

"Larkspur, dear," she says in greeting. She's wearing a green floral housedress and pink slippers.

"Hi, Mrs. Huttle. I just wanted to say hello, since I haven't seen you lately."

"Hard to see me when you keep yourself so busy."

I feel like I should apologize, but really, for what?

"Larkspur, I'm *glad* to see you've been busy."

"Oh!" And I'm relieved she cleared that up, because I had no idea that's what she meant.

"There was a long time where you kept yourself as isolated as I did. And that's not good for a young lady."

I nod, since she's right.

"Larkspur, I have a favor to ask you."

"Sure, Mrs. Huttle." Favors I can do—talking about life with Mrs. Huttle, well that's much harder.

"You can start calling me *Ms.* Huttle."

"Uh, yes, ma'am."

"I'm not going to be keeping to myself that much anymore, either. I've placed an ad with ChristianSeniors.com, and the responses from hot men are pouring in." She laughs and slaps the white wooden doorframe at my expression. *Hot men?*

"Mrs.—*Ms.* Huttle, are you sure they're, I don't know, safe?"

"Not a bit. And that's half the fun! Now you get out of here, because I have a date to get ready for."

"You shouldn't meet them here, you know," I call, before she can shut the door in my face.

151

LARKSPUR

"Now, Larkspur, I've known you since you were in kindergarten." She looks at me sternly, and it's enough to make me wish I hadn't said anything. "When I want your advice, I will let you know. I have lived much longer than you and I do not need you telling me how and when to conduct my business."

"Oh, Ms. Huttle, I just—"

"I don't want to hear it." This time she slams the door in my face, and I don't say anything else.

I step off the porch and am almost around the corner of the house when she opens the door and calls me again. "Larkspur!"

"Yes, ma'am?"

"Thank you for caring, you nosy girl." It's said begrudgingly, but I don't care. My heart swells that she bothered to say it at all. I start to say, "You're welcome," but she's already slammed the door again.

And really, who can blame her? She has a hot date tonight. At least she probably won't have to deal with the guy's overbearing mother, I think, with a smile.

So, what to wear? After 20 minutes of staring at my open closet and not moving from my perch on the edge of the bed, I call Christine.

She arrives with an armful of clothes, which I didn't expect, and a bottle of nail polish, which I totally did expect.

"What's it called?"

"Simply Primp. Which is why I had to bring it, of course, not that we have time to use it now."

"I know. I stared at my closet and wasted lots of time I could have been spending strategizing what to do when Mrs. Stephens says, 'Larkspuuur,' and then tells me all the ways I'm wrong for Brant."

"Oh, please, Lark. She's not that bad. I kind of liked her when we had breakfast."

"That was not her. That was the jeans and Birkenstocks version, and she said I was ugly when you and Brant weren't listening. The one I know would have called me ugly while wearing silk and a chignon."

"Well, you'll figure it out when that happens. But for now, let's pick out what you'll wear. Sorry, I don't have a silk pantsuit for you to borrow. Wouldn't it have been cute for you to match?"

I give Christine a look that expresses clearly my opinion of that suggestion, and she tosses me a skirt and top I've never seen her in.

"Is this new?"

"No. Yes. Sort of—I bought it when I thought I was going to lose 10 pounds, and then I didn't."

I give Christine the same look, since the thought of her needing to lose 10 pounds is as stupid as me showing up to dinner in a silk pantsuit.

"Anyway, it's adorable, and perfect, so go try it on."

The brown corduroy skirt is a good length on me, and the top is an aqua three quarter-sleeved number with a little bit of crochet work around the neckline.

When I come out of the bathroom, Christine's face lights up. "Oh it fits! You look great."

I give a twirl, and she's right. Nothing in my own closet would have worked this well.

Christine tosses me a flower pin in the same brown as the skirt. "Try this." She laughs. "That pin might even be silk!"

"So what are you doing tonight?" I ask, noticing that Christine is dressed up a little more than usual.

"Going out with one of the single moms from my StrollerMama class. She said she needed a night out with another grown-up, and it sounded fun."

I refrain from asking about Chad, the Unattractive.

"Good. Guess who else has plans tonight?"

Christine thinks for a minute before saying, "I don't know."

"Ms. Huttle."

"Yeah? What's she doing?"

"Hot date with a guy she met on ChristianSeniors.com. She placed an ad!"

"Nooo! Mrs. Huttle?"

"Now it's *Ms.* Huttle."

"Wow. Hey, I better go so I'm not here when your dinner companions arrive, Larkspuuur!" Christine hugs me and swipes a bottle of nail polish from my dining room table as she skips out the door.

I feel like throwing up when Brant knocks on the door. He's alone,

LARKSPUR

which is a good start, and it does a lot to ease the wave of nausea I'm experiencing. He tells me his mom is meeting us at the restaurant. I let out a breath, glad to hear that I have another 15 minutes.

Brant gives my hand a squeeze, and whispers into my ear, "You look pretty." I have no idea why he whispered it, but it gives me goose bumps anyway.

I don't ask where we're going, since location isn't really the make or break detail here. How incredibly angry and nasty Mrs. Stephens will be is the make or break detail, and whatever we might eat pales in comparison to that awful truth. And how can she not be nasty to me, after what Brant told me he said to her?

Seafood. I should have known. Brant, desert boy from landlocked Plains Point, Texas, has discovered a passion for seafood. We've just sat down next to one another in a booth when Mrs. Stephens arrives and tosses her little silk purse into the other side of the booth before sliding in.

"Brant. Larkspuuur." The look of triumph on her face the other night at the Italian restaurant is gone. I'm thrilled at this, but also nervous at the determined look she wears in its place. The silk pantsuit of choice is red, and I decide she means it as a show of her feminine, maternal power. I've seen her in many a silk pantsuit, and once in jeans—but never in the color red.

"Hello, Mom."

"Hi, Mrs. Stephens."

Big, big awkward pause.

"I understand that my son is willing to throw away his life for you, Larkspuuur."

"Mom!"

How romantic.

"I don't know what you've been doing to inspire that sort of dedication, but perhaps you should consider if it's wise."

"What I've been—doing?"

"Yes, dear. Normally males of any species make ridiculously poor choices when feminine…wiles…are in the picture."

Wow, she's direct. And, okay, she was eloquent about it, but she just called me a tramp.

I steal a sideways look at Brant, whose eyes are wide, and his mouth is a little open, too. Who can blame the guy for being too shocked to ride to my rescue here?

"Mrs. Stephens. I have not done what it appears you are accusing me of—not even close." I momentarily get a little thrill from the realization that she thinks I have "wiles" of the feminine sort. Me! Ha! But then, that was merely her delicate way of accusing me of seducing her son, and I must not fall for her petty insults. "Perhaps Brant is not throwing away his life by spending time in my company, and maybe his choices are not 'ridiculously poor.'"

The waitress asks what we'd like, and I say, "Coconut shrimp" without ever having looked at the menu to see if it's there. But I don't want that waitress walking away to give us more time, either, so my answer forces Brant and Mrs. Stephens into a decision as well.

"Oysters. Definitely."

Mrs. Stephens asks for a house salad and adds that she won't be staying long since she's already lost most of her appetite. I think she looks at Brant to see if this elicits sympathy, which it does not.

I watch the waitress leave, regretting that she wasn't more chatty.

"I've presented you with many more appealing, more suitable women than Larkspuuur, Brant. Monique is an up-and-coming attorney. Danica has talent and connections in the entertainment industry."

I swallow a lemon seed from my iced water and cough. Or maybe it's only the thought that Mrs. Stephens is really saying that Danica is more suitable than I am because of her "talent." Oh, that's funny. Really, I'd like to be shooting pigeons with Stanley right now. Seems like an excellent thing to be doing, instead of sitting here accidentally eating lemon seeds.

Mrs. Stephens continues, "You haven't appreciated my efforts, and are being stubborn so that I'll be hurt. You've gone back on your word, and I never thought I'd say that about you."

"Well, maybe it was a 'word' I never should have given. I'm sorry I ever said your approval would be that important to me." Brant takes a sip of water and replaces his glass carefully. "Because it's *not*."

I give a small gasp, as does Mrs. Stephens. "Brant!"

"It's not, Mom. I said that to you when you were going through a

LARKSPUR

rough time, and I would have said anything then to make you happy. But I'm not going to live the rest of my life based on what you do and do not approve of, and who you think is 'suitable.'"

I squeeze his hand under the table to thank him.

"Listen, Mom, Lark is who I find appealing and suitable."

Okay, little bit of a blush there. Let's not go declaring me appealing to your mom, Brant. Kinda awkward, especially when she'd like to kill me.

"Not anyone else. If you want to spend time with me, you're going to treat her with the respect she deserves. Can you do that?"

Mrs. Stephens looks at me, and her mouth forms a single line. Her eyes narrow, like she has me in the crosshairs of one of Stanley's guns. Finally, she speaks. "Not tonight. Maybe not ever."

"Then we're done for tonight, and maybe forever."

"You don't mean that."

"I do, actually. I love this amazing woman, and I don't see that changing anytime soon."

I squeeze my own hand, just to release some serious nervous energy.

Mrs. Stephens gets very still at this declaration, leans across the table toward me, and in a low voice says, "You will never, ever be good enough for him."

I bite the inside of my top lip, holding it closed. *So* badly I want to lean back across the table and in the same low voice say, "Neither will you." But I don't, in a showing of self-control I am greatly proud of. Then that moment passes, and I wonder if I'm proud of that self-control, or if I'll regret not saying it later.

Brant stands and silently waits for his mother to do the same. She drags her gaze from me, gets her purse, and leaves without another word. Brant sits down beside me again, shoulders slumped.

"You okay?" I ask. It isn't difficult to see that this dinner was a lot harder on him than it was on me. In a way he just lost his mother, gave her up really, for me. I simply dodged a few insults, and the two don't really compare.

"I'm great." He turns to me and kisses me with more affection than is appropriate for a crowded restaurant.

"What was that?"

"I love you. And I've tried to make that all right with her. That's all I needed to do. If she can't handle this, then she can't. But I'm not going to miss out on anything else that has to do with you." He looks at me intently. "I want it all."

I laugh, partly relieved that it's just us, and partly because of what he said. "Uh huh."

He turns a little pink. "I didn't mean that. Well, okay, I *did* mean that. But I didn't mean to say it."

"Brant you need to be careful," I say to him, looking into his eyes. "Males can make ridiculously poor choices when faced with feminine wiles."

He leans forward and kisses me again. "We can. She was so right about that one little thing. So watch those wiles, okay?"

21

Sasha is standing at my desk, smiling at me, but I don't know why. Since she never stands at my desk, smiling or not, I think Brenda must have said something about my wanting her job.

"Hi."

"Hi, Lark. Could you come back to my office when you get a minute?"

"Uh huh."

She leaves, still smiling, and I go to see Brenda.

"Brenda! Did you say something to Sasha?"

"Maybe."

"Brenda!"

"You know how it is here. Management is so weird and artsy, and they want you to find your own replacement if you go on vacation, or even if you quit they want your ideas on who to interview. That's how John was able to hire you. Same thing. So when Sasha asked if I knew anyone, I told her."

"So she *is* quitting?"

"Yeah, she wants to move to Houston to be near her family. She just doesn't want it to get to management that she's quitting before she's had a chance to find someone. I think you're it."

"Really, you do?"

"Yeah, which is bad for me, really."

"Why?"

"I was hoping I could talk you into taking my job."

"You're quitting, too?" And this makes no sense at all, especially since I am not an art teacher.

"Just temporarily. You know, maternity leave."

I squeal. Like a big happy pig friend, I squeal...probably what she wanted me to do, so I'm glad. She returns my hug, and tells me to go talk to Sasha and we can talk later.

"You want to go shopping later?"

"Sure, what are you buying?"

"A baby frontpack."

"A what?"

"You know, it looks like a backpack, but you wear it in front and you stick a baby in it."

"Oh. Huh."

"They have really cute leather ones, and I can't wait to see Carl in one."

"Right. Okay. Baby frontpack shopping. Everything just changed, huh?"

"Yeah. Everything did."

"Congratulations."

∼

I am air-drying my toenails by lying on the living room floor and sticking them up in the direction of the air-conditioning vent. They're taking forever to dry, but I'm in a lazy mood anyway so I don't mind. They're painted Pretty Girl, which I got only for the name—the color is redder than I usually like. But I have an important dinner date with Brant and Mama and Stanley coming up, and Pretty Girl seemed a good choice.

While staring at my Pretty Girl toes, it occurs to me that Mrs. Stephens has done me a huge favor. And not only by acting like such a moron that now we're practically assured of no contact, but by presenting Brant with all those "appealing" options. I mean, I was so insecure about not looking a certain way, and by accident she proved to me that when given all those other choices, Brant still would pick me. I don't think I ever would have had the confidence to assume that. I always would have wondered what would have happened if the opportunities arose with more classically pretty girls. And he had opportunity after opportunity, and wasn't ever interested, except in an attempt to please his mother. That is priceless information that most girlfriends don't have.

Mama calls right as I'm expecting Brant to arrive.

"Lark, baby. I need to know something."

"Yeah?"

"Is Brant going to propose to you tonight? If so, I need to start preparing myself now."

"We're not, um, really at that point, Mama."

"You sure?"

"Oh yeah. I think you sort of know these things, and we're not there."

"Okay. Just needed to know what to wear. I'll go change into something not as nice."

"Right."

I hang up, wondering what the outfit for such an occasion would be and realizing Mama is much more nervous about this dinner than I am. I've grown pretty fond of Stanley lately. Now that Mama and I are doing better, there hasn't been a reason to be nervous around her.

We meet at a place that Stanley suggested, and the walls are covered in mounted fish and deer. "Good home cookin' here, Lark." He nods as he looks around with approval.

We're shown to a table and the waiter arrives with four iced teas, not that anyone ordered them. It's just the sort of place where they assume everyone likes iced tea.

Brant and Stanley sit across the table from one another, and Mama and I sit across from each other. She keeps dropping her napkin and fiddling with her menu, and I can't remember ever seeing her nervous before.

We order, all starting with the phrase "chicken-fried" since almost everything on the menu is chicken-fried something or other. Brant and Stanley talk about the current projects they're helping with at church, and Mama leans over to me.

"Are you sure I'm, you know, wearing the *right* outfit?"

"Yeah, Mama. Save that other one. Really."

She loosens up a little after that, but I wonder why she even thinks that should anyone be proposing to me, she'd definitely be there and need a certain dress in the first place.

Then I get distracted, wondering again about what *I* would wear. And then I get to wondering about Brenda, who wore a stained T-shirt.

"So, Mrs. Andrews, I was wondering how Lark got her name," Brant says.

"Call me Gracie." She moves her mouth to the left, like she does when she's thinking sometimes. I don't think she's thinking about her answer, though, but *if* she'll answer at all. I hope so.

I've always hated my name and the one time I remember asking her this question, I didn't get an answer. Mama said something briefly about weeds and left the room, and I never asked again.

"The spring before I got pregnant with Lark her father and I moved into a house over on Fifteenth Street. And there was this enormous flowerbed out front, and it was filled with what must have been tens of thousands of little weeds. I thought if I could pull them up when they were little, I could stay on top of it. So I went out every night and pulled them. But the job got away from me, and there were too many, and they took over."

I'm looking around the table, wondering if Stanley and Brant wonder if she's lost her mind as well.

"So I gave up on the weeds. Not long after that Lark's dad left and I found out I was pregnant. I was devastated. I didn't want a baby then, of course, but I had one."

Our food arrives then, and Mama pauses for the waiter to place our chicken-fried everything in front of us. Stanley prays, and then Mama begins her story where she left off.

"In late May I went outside and that entire flower bed was in bloom. What I had thought were weeds turned out to be the most beautiful bluish-purple flowers. Thousands of them—so many that people would stop on the street to admire them. My neighbor told me they were larkspur. When it came time for Lark to be born, I still didn't have a name. I held her for the first time and remembered those flowers. How at first I'd not recognized their purpose and beauty and tried to uproot them. Then how they lived and blessed everyone who saw them anyway. That was how you were, and that's how you got your name, baby."

Tears are in my eyes. There's something beautiful in what she's said, but still, Mama thought I was a weed in her life, and I can't get past that yet.

LARKSPUR

"Thanks for telling me that, Gracie," Brant says and squeezes my hand under the table. It's a nice hand squeeze that says, "I know you're not a weed." At least, I think that's what it says. Maybe it says, "Sorry, but your mother is so crazy that I can now never pass on her genetic material to our offspring."

"You're welcome. Aren't you glad they weren't heliotrope, baby?"

"Or hollyhocks," says Stanley with a smile and a wink in my direction. Stanley—a wink! I laugh at him and give Mama the smile she's waiting for.

"Hollyhock," I say. "Yeah, that would have gotten me made fun of even more than Larkspur did."

Brant clears his throat, purposefully. Mama sits up straighter, and Stanley puts down his fork.

"I want you two to hear something, and I wanted to invite you here tonight for this." Brant looks at me and takes my hand and looks back across the table at Stanley and Mama.

At that moment Mama kicks my shin so hard that I double over in pain, my nose inches from my corn. The corn looks really gross this close up, and I focus my watering eyes on the individual specks of pepper on the kernels, while I try to sit up and refrain from kicking her back. I manage to reign in that urge, barely, but only after reminding myself that she just had a heart attack. She looks wide-eyed and apologetic, so I glare at her and turn to Brant.

"I-I wanted you to know that I love Lark."

It almost makes the throbbing in my right shin seem far away. It totally sends me into that place where I silently thank Jesus over and over.

Mama and I smile at Brant, and Stanley says, "Yep. Reckoned ya did, son."

Two days later Tom pulls me over. I get the throw-up feeling again, like last time, but now it's because I'm afraid of what he'll do. An insanely jealous po-lice officer, who will never make detective, and there aren't any witnesses around. This is one of those times I wish I weren't always swept up in the pretty exterior packages that sometimes conceal really unattractive men.

"Lark."

"Hi, Tom. Was I speeding?"

"Nope. Just wanted to introduce you to someone. This is Julia. Julia Sather," he says, as if this should mean something to me.

And that does sound familiar, vaguely, but I'm suddenly remembering the lyrics in an old Paul Simon song: "She was a roly-poly, little bat-faced girl." I'd always wondered what someone with that description would look like, and now I think I know.

"Uh, nice to meet you."

Julia smiles and hides behind Tom, as if I'm going to do her evil. Or, come to think of it, as if she read my awful thoughts, and now I feel bad.

"Julia loves to bake. She has all her grandmother's recipes." Tom smiles, puts his arm around her, and they walk back to his car.

A small surprised sound, almost like a gasp, escapes me as they shut their doors and Tom drives by, flashing a triumphant grin.

"That is a mean, mean man," I say aloud to myself, envisioning the golden dew drops on the pies that Julia's grandmother makes. Julia, who probably knows the mystery behind those little drops of gold, amazing girlfriend potential for anyone at First Lutheran just because of her possession of her grandmother's cooking secrets. *Well, looks aren't everything, Lark, and that was proof right there.* And on that note, I wonder when Christine will let me meet Chad, Not Cad.

I'm left reeling that Tom could successfully get back at me by making me salivate over chocolate pie that I will never again taste— pie that he is apparently eating as a perk of dating the roly poly, little bat-faced girl. That took some thinking that I hadn't thought he was capable of, that's for sure. At least now I know why he isn't busy pulling over Brant anymore. He's not plotting his revenge any longer; he's eating it regularly for dessert.

I walk into Brant's and tell him about getting pulled over.

"Was the pie really that good, Lark? I mean, it's just pie."

"No, you don't understand. It was really that good."

We paint, and we paint, and when we're finished, Brant's house looks

LARKSPUR

like the final two glorious pages in *Mabel and the Rainbow*. The walls are alive with the colors in life that Brant loves. He had trouble deciding on what color to paint the last room, and I was surprised when one day I came over to find he'd already started with a shade of yellow.

"What is it?"

"Guess."

"It's a butterscotch candy."

"Nope."

I start rolling the paint on the wall behind his bed.

"It's a color in a sunrise?"

"No."

"Last guess. It's what you get when you mix two of your other favorite colors?"

"It's this," he says, putting down his roller and coming over to me. With one hand he gently twirls a lock of my hair between his finger, and watches my face until I say, "Oh."

"You're painting your bedroom the color of my hair?"

"Yes. It's gold, but with red in it, too. Beautiful, like you are."

"It's a good thing I love you."

"Why's that?"

"Because that would be really creepy, and not romantic at all if I didn't. Ha! It wasn't that long ago you compared my hair to your old, sick cat, and here you are painting your bedroom the same color!"

"You love me enough to forgive me for that?"

"I do."

"Good."

"What's the name of that song you like…?"

"Trashy Women?" He grins.

"No! The one about shutting up…?"

"Oooh. That one." He pulls me closer and whispers, "Shut Up and Kiss Me."

About the Author

KELSEY KILGORE makes her home in windswept West Texas with her three boys, two dogs, and one cat. She's the writer behind the award-winning blog *HolyMama,* candid reflections on her life and family. She appreciates small details and delights in bringing them to life in works of fiction, often with humor.

Whenever possible, she's lifting weights at the gym, off-roading in her big pickup, wakeboarding, kickboxing, or engaging in other exceptionally ladylike endeavors. Next on her list of activities to try are rappelling, parasailing, surfing, and possibly cooking. She is a fan of eBay, colorful shoes, fantastically designed jeans, and long candlelit baths.

http://holymama.org/ ▪ www.oaktara.com

falling in love

Hopeful Romances for Hopeless Romantics.

Unforgettable romances that will make you fall in love again… or for the first time. Available in Contemporary, Historical, Prairie, Amish, Western, and other flavors.

falling in love
CONTEMPORARY

Happily Ever After
SERIES

Who doesn't dream of happily ever after?

The Happily Ever After series highlights three contemporary women who are searching for their love-of-a-lifetime, complete with unconditional love, heart-warming acceptance, and toe-tingling romance.

Melody goes on her dream vacation trip and finds her dream guy—someone who is truly all she has ever hoped for, and more. But a surprising secret pulls them apart until she comes to a stunning realization that will transform her heart…and change her life forever.

Larkspur, fed up with dating losers and short on time while juggling several jobs, finds herself on a whirlwind ride of dates she allows her meddling mama to set up. Yet her heart is strangely tugged toward the neighbor who has driven her crazy all her life.

Evie is already in love with the man she's sure she's going to marry. But Ben is not her parents' choice. When they push her to consider an arranged marriage with Eli, their handsome family lawyer, which man will Evie choose? Is it possible to find the man you truly love while you're dating another?

All three women discover that true love doesn't always match what you plan, and it can be in a form much different from what you've imagined, but it can be better than you could ever dream.

Melody

JEN MELLAND

HAPPILY EVER AFTER

What if she met the man of her dreams... on her dream vacation?

Melody Kennedy just wants to get away and relax before the pressures of life hit again. A trip to Jamaica with her best friend seems like the perfect antidote. Sun, sandy beaches, her favorite books, and who knows? She might even meet her true love there. A girl can dream, right?

Then she runs—literally—into Jude Deveraux, a smart, handsome man with an intriguing British accent. He seems to like her, but is he too good to be true? And what about Mike, the guy who has his eye on her friend Ros? Could this be the two friends' time to find real, lasting love?

Melody is determined that this vacation will have a happily-ever-after ending...but it might be very different from the one she plans.

A whirlwind romance in an exotic setting that will make you fall in love again...or for the first time.

Evie

HILARY HAMBLIN

HAPPILY EVER AFTER

Caught between the love of two men, how will she choose?

Evie's wealthy parents have just given her an ultimatum: stop dating her boyfriend Ben, or lose their financial support her junior year of college. Worse, they want her to consider an arranged marriage to the family lawyer, Eli Wheatly. True, Eli is handsome—tall, with a mop of curly black hair—but looks aren't enough for Evie. She dreams of true love.

When Evie and Ben hatch a scheme to continue quietly dating while she goes out on a few dates with Eli to keep her parents happy, Evie is surprised and confused by the romantic flutterings she feels around Eli. What if she's found the man she truly loves…while dating another?

A beautiful small-town romance that will make you fall in love again…or for the first time.

Maple City Chapel Library
2015 Lincolnway East
Goshen, IN 46526